Also edited by Donald R. Gallo

SIXTEEN:
Short Stories by Outstanding
Writers for Young Adults

VISIONS:
Nineteen Short Stories by Outstanding
Writers for Young Adults

CONNECTIONS:
Short Stories by Outstanding
Writers for Young Adults

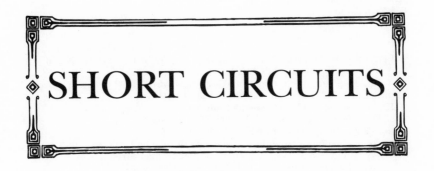

SHORT CIRCUITS

Thirteen
Shocking Stories
by
Outstanding Writers
for Young Adults

Edited by
DONALD R. GALLO

Delacorte
Press

Published by
Delacorte Press
Bantam Doubleday Dell Publishing Group, Inc.
666 Fifth Avenue
New York, New York 10103

A portion of this book's royalties, earmarked for research in young adult literature, will go to the Assembly on Literature for Adolescents of the National Council of Teachers of English (ALAN).

Library of Congress Cataloging in Publication Data

Short circuits : thirteen shocking stories by outstanding writers for young adults / edited by Donald R. Gallo.
    p.   cm.
    Summary: Includes offerings from Joan Lowery Nixon, Vivien Alcock, Robert Westall, and Joan Aiken.
    ISBN 0-385-30785-3
    1. Horror tales, American. 2. Horror tales, English. 3. Ghost stories, American. 4. Ghost stories, English. [1. Horror stories. 2. Ghosts—Fiction. 3. Short stories.]   I. Gallo, Donald R.
    PZ5.S558 1992
    [Fic]—dc20   91-46164
                                                  CIP
                                                     AC

Manufactured in the United States of America

November 1992

10 9 8 7 6 5 4 3 2 1

BVG

For M. Jerry Weiss
with thanks
for all he has done
to promote YA books

CONTENTS

ZAPPED

INTRODUCTION

Scaring my younger sister was one of my favorite activities when I was a teenager. I'd hide in closets and jump out at her with a yell as she opened the door. I'd slither under her bed when she wasn't in the room and moan or make strange screeching noises when she came near. She always reacted predictably: screaming first and then yelling, "Mommy, he's scaring me again!"

But I never liked to be scared myself. I entered darkened rooms by announcing, "I know you're in here," whether I knew someone was hiding in there or not. I avoided seeing creepy horror films and never read a book designed to send shivers down a reader's spine. Stephen King, of course, wasn't writing back then, nor had Freddy Krueger been conceived.

I still avoid frightening stories and horror movies—real life is scary enough for me. And supernatural occurrences depicted in books and on film or video seem too farfetched for my rational approach to life. But I know how strongly teenagers are attracted to those kinds of stories. My own son will watch one frightful video after another, replaying the goriest parts again and again.

You can thus understand that it was only reluctantly that I agreed to compile a collection of horror/supernatural stories. Not being a devotee of that genre, I wasn't sure I could adequately judge the quality of such stories. Then again, I decided that if *I* enjoyed the stories, they had to be good.

So I contacted a number of writers who are well-known by teenage readers for their horror or supernatural stories, authors such as Joan Aiken, Joan Lowery Nixon, and Robert Westall. I also invited a few other authors who write for teenagers but who have not yet become as well-known as those on the previous list. Each author was asked to write a story that focused on a teenage character and that was creepy, scary, weird, horrifying, or shocking in some way. The resulting stories, as you will see, are very interesting.

If you are looking for lots of gore, though, you won't find it here. Instead, you will be surprised at the amount of humor in many of these original stories. Oh, don't worry: there are some stories in this book that will terrify you, some that will horrify you, others that will make you grimace, and one that is really gruesome. There are several ghost stories and one story set in the future. A couple of the stories will make you smile with relief at the outcome. Most others will increase your pulse rate, create tension, and build suspense right up to the frightful conclusion.

Be prepared to be jolted, electrified, and zapped as you read these shocking stories.

JOLTED

Life was awfully dull for Laurie until she arrived at her eccentric grandaunt's home in New Orleans. There someone else wanted the house for herself. . . .

THERE'S A TOMB WAITING FOR YOU

JOAN LOWERY NIXON

This is my favorite part of the house. Here, at the north window in the spare bedroom on the top floor, I can look beyond the thick branches of dusty oaks, beyond the spear-tipped points on the wrought-iron fence, to the tentlike roofs of the tombs in the cemetery across the street.

The whitewashed tombs, their brick walls crumbling in decay —like the bodies long-ago laid inside them—both fascinate and terrify me. Vivienne has plans that involve my being there, but I have my own thoughts about that.

I don't think I like Vivienne very much.

Laurie Reynolds plopped onto the narrow bed, a notepad and pen in one hand, and gazed around the small bedroom. It was exquisite in every way, from the antique silver-backed mirror and brush on the dark cherry dresser to the curlicues on the brass headboard. It was obvious that her grandaunt Vivienne had worked very hard and used a great deal of her latest ex-husband's money to buy and redo her New Orleans house. But it was overdone, much like Vivienne.

With a sigh Laurie brushed back her straight, dark hair and pulled one leg up, crossing it over the other to make a rest for the notepad. She'd arrived in New Orleans yesterday, and she hadn't written to her parents—even though she'd promised to write the minute she'd settled in—because there was nothing to say.

There was really nothing about her life—here or anywhere else—that was important enough to write about. At home it was the same thing every day—school, homework, going to the mall with her friends. Laurie didn't date much. She never knew what to say to a guy on a date, and it was horrible being swallowed by an embarrassing, awkward silence because there was absolutely nothing to talk about.

Candy Phillips, her best friend, had tried to encourage her. "Laurie," she'd said, "you've got to let guys know you're *interesting*!" But Laurie didn't know how to be interesting.

"Laurie, dear, sometimes you have to take the initiative," Mom had told her, but the idea of taking the initiative about anything was too impossible for Laurie to even consider.

Then Mom got the gruesome idea that maybe Laurie's vistas should be broadened—as she put it—and since summer vacation had begun, how nice it would be for Laurie if she spent a month with Aunt Vivienne in her beautiful new remodeled town home in old New Orleans. Laurie had protested that she didn't even like her mother's aunt Vivienne very much, but her mother had been so excited about the idea, Laurie didn't have a choice.

Twice Vivienne had visited the Reynoldses at their home in Ventura, and Laurie had not been impressed. Vivienne Adoue—former New York actress with dyed-orange hair, delicately tended skin, and long, black artificial lashes—liked to wear bright, flowing things she called caftans and tons of rings and bracelets, and she always spoke with rounded tones as though she were on the stage.

Laurie winced as she thought of spending the next four weeks with her grandaunt. It wasn't just Vivienne's show of resigned patience at having Laurie as a guest, it was her weird plan that called for Laurie to work under the miserably hot summer sun in a cemetery.

"I'm going to be just the teensiest bit immodest and tell you that the cemetery renovation was my own wonderful idea," Vivienne had said enthusiastically. "The poor little cemetery has been left unattended for so long and is in such miserable condition. If the city can't care for it, then its neighbors can. I invited everyone who lives in the vicinity to meet, adopt a tomb, and work to repair it, and we had a wonderful turnout for the first go-round." Her smile was brilliant. "I knew you'd want to be an enthusiastic part of the project, Laurie, so I saved a tomb just for you."

Laurie hadn't been able to pretend enthusiasm. As a matter of fact she couldn't help shuddering and knew she had offended Vivienne. With all her heart Laurie wanted to be home in California. The most horrible thing she could think of was to be here in New Orleans, adopting a tomb.

Laurie's thoughts were interrupted as Vivienne called her to dinner, and after the meal, when they had settled somewhat uncomfortably on two silk-upholstered love seats, Laurie tried to make amends for her earlier behavior.

"I guess it's just something I've never thought about— caring for tombs," she said. "In California the only cemeteries I've seen look like grass-covered hills and have nothing but flat plaques to mark the graves."

Vivienne placed her fragile coffee cup on an equally fragile table and said, "In New Orleans the water level is so high that the deceased have to be buried above-ground. And that's why houses here don't have cellars. They'd be filled with water."

"But you have a cellar," Laurie blurted out.

Vivienne explained, "Obviously you didn't pay attention to the structure of my town house when you arrived, but take a close look tomorrow. You'll see that we have a half-flight of stairs from the street to our front door. Our first floor is really a second floor because underneath it is an unfinished area made of cement and brick. My architect did whatever had to be done to shore up and strengthen the walls and floor, then put in the furnace, the water heater, and the air conditioner." She paused. "That room is where my workmen found the skeleton— buried inside a small crypt made of bricks, way back in the far corner."

Laurie sat upright. "You found a skeleton? Of a—a person? I mean, a real person?"

"The workmen found it . . . or her, I suppose I should say."

"Her?"

"Well, naturally we called the police, and they called in a medical examiner, and I practically hounded the dear man until he gave me his findings because, after all, I had just bought the house, and in a way I felt that the skeleton belonged to me."

"Nobody ever told me about the skeleton," Laurie said. "Not even once. Not ever. Does Mom know about it?"

Vivienne shrugged and swept the skirt of her deep-blue caftan to one side. "Probably not," she said. "I may be the world's worst correspondent."

"Do they know who she was? The skeleton, that is?"

"No, just that she was female and probably in her late teens and had been murdered. There was a rusty old knife lying between the broken bones of her rib cage and a few of those horrid voodoo things next to it."

Laurie shivered. "What are voodoo things?"

"Superstitious, magic charms that are supposed to have powers for good or evil—in this case a little bag of powders and the stub of a black candle. If there was anything else with the body, I don't remember. Naturally I tossed out all that dreadful voodoo clutter as quickly as possible."

"What did it mean?" Laurie asked.

"I don't know, and I don't want to know. Voodoo was once very powerful here in all classes of society, and I'm glad it no longer is."

"You mean everyone stopped using voodoo? Why?"

Vivienne tapped her fingers impatiently on the arm of her chair. "I didn't say *everyone,* Laurie. It's easy enough to find stores that still sell voodoo things to superstitious people, especially in the Quarter."

Laurie tried to picture the crypt, and her questions tumbled out. "Did they know whose skeleton it was? Did they find out the girl's name? Or when the murder happened? Did they find out who killed her?"

Vivienne waved her hands before her eyes, as though trying to ward off an attack. "Stop, stop, stop! I can't possibly answer all those questions. No one can. The skeleton must have been there a long, long time. The house is *very* old, you know."

Laurie settled back and waited five seconds before she asked, "Where is her skeleton now?"

Vivienne gracefully inclined her head and smiled, in the way she must have once smiled to a front-row admirer. "It's buried in the cemetery across the street, at my own expense. Oh, I had to cut through some perfectly ridiculous red tape, but I was determined to win, and fortunately a darling judge agreed with me. The skeleton was in my house, so it's *mine*."

HER skeleton? Who does Vivienne think she is to be so posses-sive about something that belongs to someone else?
Vivienne can be very irritating.

Laurie hugged her shoulders, rubbing her arms. The air-conditioning must have been set quite high, because the house was terribly cold. Vivienne seemed to be wait-ing for Laurie's praise, so Laurie said, "It was kind of you to give the girl a final resting place."

"A final resting place?" Vivienne rolled her eyes. "Oh, if that were only so! The skeleton was buried, but I'm afraid, my dear, that the ghost walks."

The chill of the room was increasing. Laurie's words came out as a hoarse whisper as she asked, "What do you mean, Aunt Vivienne?"

Vivienne's eyes widened. "What do I mean? Well, you'll find out soon enough, Laurie, that my lovely house is haunted."

I wish Vivienne wouldn't do that—talk about skeletons and ghosts as though they were nothing more than a ghoulish mass with no soul or spirit, as though at one time they hadn't been living human beings. Why couldn't she say "the girl who lived in this house"? Or even "the poor girl who went through the horror of being murdered"?
I really don't like Vivienne.

* * *

As Laurie nervously prepared for bed, her glance flickered from side to side, watching for any silent, stealthy movement. She'd been too startled to ask Vivienne the right questions. Had the ghost ever appeared? What did the ghost do when she haunted the house? Did she show her presence by creating a breeze through the curtains at a closed window or causing a door to slowly creak open when no one was there?

Nervously Laurie's gaze swung toward the door, but the absurdity of what she was doing made her giggle, and she collapsed on the edge of the bed. She was allowing her own imagination to go as far afield as Vivienne's. This whole situation couldn't be real—an elderly, dramatic grandaunt who had found the skeleton of a murdered girl in her house, who was haunted by a ghost, and who brought the neighbors together for tomb parties. It would be something to laugh over with Candy. It really was funny . . . wasn't it?

Laurie turned off the lamp and pulled open the drapes at the window. The streetlights highlighted the dusty strands of tattered moss that hung in clumps from the massive branches of the oaks. She hated the moss. It made the trees look as though they were too old to go on living—as though they were already decaying, and their bark and limbs were dropping off in ragged lumps.

Suddenly Laurie froze, not from the frosty breath that blew against the back of her neck but from a hideous evil that slithered around her, tickling her nostrils with a sour stench and creeping over her body like a blanket of furry gray mildew. She tensed, straining to listen for what would come next, but her heart pounded so loudly against her eardrums, it blotted out all other sound.

There was no question in Laurie's mind that the ghost

was in the room. What did she want of Laurie? What was she going to do?

Laurie whirled—clutching the draperies for support—and peered into the darkness, but there was nothing to see. "Who are you?" she whispered.

The air ruffled, sucking the horror toward the door.

"What do you want?" Laurie demanded.

She waited, but the air had stilled.

"Are you there?" Laurie asked, her heart still beating loudly, but the room was once more quiet and peaceful, and she knew the ghost had left.

Laurie trembled as she climbed into bed, wondering about this girl who haunted Vivienne's house. Were there good ghosts and bad ghosts, and was this a bad one? Laurie had felt the terror of the evil that surrounded her and knew, without understanding why, that this girl-ghost had once been party to some horrible things. What had she been like when she was alive? Why was she haunting the house where she'd been murdered? Why had she been murdered?

I'll never be able to sleep, Laurie thought, but as the sun woke her the next morning, she realized with surprise that she had slept soundly.

"Tell me more about the ghost," Laurie said as she met Vivienne for breakfast.

"There's nothing to tell." Vivienne pulled two slices of toast from the toaster and cut them into tidy, unbuttered triangles on her own plate. "Help yourself to whatever you'd like. There's cereal and toast," she added as she gracefully slid into a chair at the kitchen table.

Laurie poured herself a large glass of orange juice and buttered two slices of raisin bread before she seated herself across from Vivienne. "What I mean is, what does the ghost do when she's haunting you?'' Laurie asked. "Do you see her? Does she tell you what she wants?''

Vivienne thought a moment. "I've never seen the ghost, thank goodness, and I haven't the vaguest notion of what she wants or why she's here.'' She peered at Laurie. "What a peculiar question.''

Laurie felt herself blushing. "I just thought maybe she'd like to leave. I mean, why hang around the place where she was murdered?''

"It's no secret that *I'd* like the ghost to leave,'' Vivienne answered. "That's why I had the skeleton buried. *Requiescat in pace,* and all that. But I should have known the ghost wouldn't go away easily, because it's so thoroughly disagreeable.''

"Disagreeable?'' Laurie murmured. That was hardly how she would have described the ghost.

Vivienne's indignation stiffened her backbone. "When I said disagreeable, that's exactly what I meant. At times the ghost is bad-tempered and unruly. It deliberately breaks things! I mean, knocking that expensive Steuben bowl off the piano! Can you believe it? And my crystal— the horrid thing smashed six goblets for no good reason at all! There's no excuse for that kind of atrocious behavior!''

"Maybe there *is* a reason,'' Laurie said.

Vivienne shrugged. "I'd be more inclined to believe there was a very good reason why the girl was murdered.''

"That's not very fair,'' Laurie began, and turned in her chair just as Vivienne's coffee cup sailed off the table, spraying Vivienne's caftan with coffee as the cup smashed on the tile floor.

"Oh!'' Laurie jumped up and grabbed a fistful of paper toweling. "I'm sorry. I didn't mean to—''

"Don't be ridiculous!'' Vivienne snapped. She

snatched the towels from Laurie and mopped at her skirt. "It wasn't *you* who threw the coffee. It was that nasty little ghost."

"Maybe the things you said—" Laurie began, but Vivienne interrupted with a scowl.

"I should be able to say whatever I like in my own house!" She looked at her wristwatch. "Gracious! If we don't hurry, we'll be late for the tomb party. Run upstairs this very minute and put on suitable clothing. Keep in mind that you're going to get hot and sweaty and very dirty."

Laurie kept her irritation with Vivienne to herself and, leaving her grandaunt to pick up the pieces of the broken cup, ran up the stairs to her room.

It's obvious that Vivienne is too selfish to consider anyone's feelings but her own. No one deserves to be murdered, no matter how evil they might have been, and no one—living or dead— deserves to be talked about with such unkindness.

It's very hard to put up with Vivienne.

Laurie had no sooner reached the top of the stairs when she heard a thump and a shriek. She raced back down and found Vivienne seated on the polished hardwood floor in the dining room, rubbing her knees and scowling. A small area rug was wadded to one side.

"How did you fall?" Laurie asked. She held out a hand to help Vivienne up.

"I didn't fall! I was pushed!" Vivienne shouted. "The stupid ghost jerked the rug right out from under me." She took Laurie's hand and struggled to her feet.

"Are you hurt?"

Her voice acid with sarcasm, Vivienne answered, "It wasn't comfortable."

"I mean, do you think you should see a doctor? Or lie down for a while?"

"Of course not. We have a tomb party to attend, if you remember. I've made sandwiches and lemonade, and when we go, you can carry the lemonade."

Vivienne attempted to edge past Laurie, but Laurie put a hand on her arm. "Have you thought about talking to someone who'd know about this kind of thing? Maybe a priest? I mean, there was a movie about exorcism. . . ."

Laurie was surprised when Vivienne looked embarrassed. "I've already considered exorcism, even though I've never been a Catholic. However, I met a bishop at a fund-raiser a few months ago, and I broached the idea to him—delicately, you understand—but he . . . would you believe that he laughed! The man actually laughed. He said nearly every old house in Louisiana claims to be haunted, and he assumed I'd like to be fashionable by being able to brag about my own ghost. He was obviously not a sympathetic type."

"But there must be something you can do," Laurie insisted, and she remembered with a shiver the evil she had experienced when she had felt the ghost's presence. "Breaking china is one thing, but trying to hurt you is something else. It's scary, Aunt Vivienne."

Vivienne drew herself up haughtily. "This is *my* house," she said. "The miserable little ghost wouldn't dare to harm me." With a sudden shooing motion she said, "Hurry and change, Laurie. The last thing I want is to be late to my party."

No. The last thing Vivienne would want would to be physically harmed. Ghosts really can harm people . . . if they want to . . . if they're evil enough.

If Vivienne weren't so wrapped up in herself, she'd have

*enough sense not to make taunting statements to a ghost who
just might take the dare.*

*Sometimes I can't stand Vivienne. It's getting awfully hard to
have to stay in the same house with her. How long am I going to
be able to take it?*

Ten neighbors met in the cemetery, under the dusty,
moss-bedraggled oaks. Most of the people who had come
were youngish or middle-aged, but there was a slow-mov-
ing, grayed, and balding man, introduced as Mr. Duhon,
who was probably even older than Vivienne.

Wearing a denim jumpsuit and a huge straw hat that
was decorated with a large silk rose, Vivienne—in her
most gracious manner—greeted each arrival with hugs
and an unwavering smile and introduced Laurie with
such enthusiasm that Laurie found herself too embarrassed to do much more than mumble hellos.

She was handed a trowel and escorted to the newest
tomb. "It needs nothing but a good weeding," Vivienne
said. "Maybe once it's spruced up, the ghost will do us all
a favor and decide to join her skeleton."

Laurie studied the whitewashed brick tomb, which
stood a little over three feet high. While the other tombs
were decorated with names and dates engraved in
stained, metal plaques or chiseled into stone blocks, this
tomb had only a plain, roughly plastered face. She wished
she knew the name of the girl whose skeleton was buried
here. That would make the job easier.

She began to dig with her trowel, tugging at loosened
clumps of weeds, but Mr. Duhon gingerly bent to examine a dirt patch in front of the tomb next to Laurie's.
"Oh-oh," he said. "See that hole? Looks to me like someone was in here getting goofer dust."

Laurie sat up and stared at him. "What?"

"Goofer dust," he said. "Dirt from a graveyard. Some people put it in gris-gris."

"W-what?" Laurie stammered again.

"For good luck," he answered, and when she continued to stare, he explained, "Gris-gris are little bags containing mixtures of things that mean good luck and ward off evil spirits."

"Is that part of voodoo?" Laurie asked.

"Good voodoo," he said.

"Do you know anyone who still believes in voodoo?"

"Oh, yes," Mr. Duhon said. Slowly, carefully, as though his bones would snap, he lowered himself to a cross-legged position on the ground. "I've never had any truck with superstition, but my sister Jennie still keeps a good-luck gris-gris in her top dresser drawer."

"But voodoo doesn't work. It couldn't. It's only superstition," Laurie said.

Mr. Duhon grinned. "If you believe it's going to work, then it works," he said. "Can't tell you how many stories I've heard over the years about people who upped and died just because they thought someone hexed 'em, or people who weren't afraid of anybody or anything because they thought they carried some kind of power around on their person."

"That's creepy," Laurie murmured.

"Don't say that to someone who believes in voodoo," Mr. Duhon said. He used his trowel to smooth dirt back into the hole, and Laurie watched him.

"You said that cemetery dirt can keep away evil spirits . . . *if* they believe in voodoo?" she asked.

"Goofer dust mixed with a few other things like ground red pepper, pieces of bone, whatever it takes."

"How do you find whatever it takes?"

He chuckled. "There are stores that sell voodoo

powders and charms all over the French Quarter. Just go in and ask. They'll tell you. Sell it to you too."

"Thanks," Laurie said, and went back to her weeding.

"Going to get rid of an evil spirit?" Mr. Duhon asked. A laugh rattled in his throat until it turned into a phlegmy cough and kept him too busy to be concerned with an answer.

Laurie worked carefully and silently and made her plans.

The exhausted workers at the tomb party, their clothes damp with sweat and streaked with grime, gave up their efforts at three o'clock and headed to their homes for hot showers.

"Isn't it all wonderful?" Vivienne said enthusiastically as she climbed the steps and unlocked the front door of her house. "I'm going to try to get a little newspaper publicity on this—only to encourage others to do the same, you understand. It's so lovely to see the tombs being repaired. We must think about planting flowers and . . ."

Laurie felt the evil surge toward them as they walked into the entry hall; but it stopped, the air swirling and shimmering as it retreated in confusion.

Vivienne stopped talking and stared at Laurie. "What is it?" she asked. "You look so odd. Are you feeling well?"

"I'm just hot," Laurie answered quickly, "and a little tired." Vivienne hadn't felt it. She hadn't stopped talking long enough to become aware.

"We all are," Vivienne said, and then she asked, "What is that you have in your hand?"

"My scarf," Laurie said.

"Is something in it?"

"Nothing important." Laurie didn't want to speak of it aloud, even though she was positive from the way the

ghost had behaved that she had felt the presence of the
goofer dust and knew what it meant. Elation became
even stronger than her fear as Laurie realized that the
ghost believed in voodoo.

"Oh, for goodness' sake!" Vivienne cried out as she
turned and went into the living room. "Will you look at
that!"

Laurie was right behind her, shocked as she saw a
heavy curio cabinet lying on the floor, the contents of its
glass shelves scattered and broken.

In tears Vivienne began to pick up the pieces while
Laurie righted the cabinet.

"I hate this ghost!" Vivienne cried. "I hate it! I hate
it!"

Laurie waited until Vivienne was calm; then she showered and dressed quickly. She left the house, her handful
of goofer dust still wrapped tightly in her scarf, and
walked three blocks to the streetcar line. After getting
directions to the French Quarter, she boarded a car and
rode to Canal Street.

As she walked into the Quarter, she kept on the look-
out for the kind of store that would sell voodoo, and it
wasn't long before she found one that seemed to be a
combination drugstore and oddities store, with a dusty
collection of bottles and jars in the window. Laurie entered the store, thankful for the coolness of the air-conditioning, and walked up to the plump woman who sat behind the counter.

"Do you . . . I mean, do you . . ." Laurie had to
clear the huskiness from her throat and try again. "Do
you sell voodoo charms here?" she asked.

The woman barely nodded. "Good voodoo only," she
said.

Laurie sighed with relief. "That's what I want," she

said. "I want to get rid of an evil spirit." She held up her scarf so the woman could see the lump in it. "I brought some goofer dust."

The woman's eyes widened. "You don't need so much," she said. "I can make you a gris-gris with just a little of what you got there." She smiled, her face cracking into pale ridges and wrinkles. "Maybe you'll give me the rest for somebody else to use? Yes?"

"I guess so," Laurie agreed.

"But gris-gris won't get rid of an evil spirit," the woman said. "It will protect you, but it won't do nothin' to make the spirit go away."

"What will?" Laurie asked.

"Brimstone," the woman said. She swayed to her feet, squeezed around one end of the counter, and clumped down the far aisle, checking each shelf until she found what she wanted. She brought three tiny yellow lumps to the counter and placed them in front of Laurie.

The odor was so pungent, Laurie's nose wrinkled. "That's sulfur," she said.

"Sulfur, brimstone, it's all the same, and it's powerful stuff. That spirit you want to get rid of, if it cast any spells, this brimstone will take them away too."

"Then that's what I want," Laurie said. "How should I use it?"

The woman reached under the counter and brought out a tiny vial of dark, oily liquid. "Put these lumps on a plate, pour this over them, and set them on fire with a match. Then you be quick to hold the plate far out in front of you, toward the spirit. You know the spirit's name?"

"No."

"Hmmm. It goes easier if you do, but that's no matter. You just say, 'Evil one, be gone with you,' and you tell it

...ienne paled, the rouge on her cheeks standing out
...ed blotches, and she murmured, "How did you
... how to do that?"

... learned," Laurie said. "I learned a lot of things
...ut voodoo." She could hear the satisfaction in her
... voice, and she could see its effect on Vivienne. Lau-
... pulled on the string around her neck, exposing the
...all bag of gris-gris. "Gris-gris for protection against evil
...irits," she said. "I dug the goofer dust for it myself."

"Oh," Vivienne whispered, and inched backward until
...er spine was pressed against the bottom stair.

Laurie smiled at Aunt Vivienne and slowly replaced the
...gris-gris under her shirt. Maybe her visit with Vivienne
...would turn out to be not so miserable after all.

A little gris-gris, a little initiative . . . Her parents had
been right about the value of initiative. Would she tell
them what had happened? Maybe, maybe not. Even
Candy probably wouldn't understand.

Tonight she might just make a list of things to say to
guys so they'd think she was interesting. It was really too
bad, Laurie thought, that her experience with a ghost
wasn't the kind of thing she could talk about on dates.

where to go, only don't tell me where you got in mind,
'cause if it's a bad place, I don't want to know about it."

"It's not a bad place," Laurie said. "I just want it to
join its skeleton in the graveyard."

"And rest easy?" The woman kept a cautious eye on
Laurie.

"Yes. And rest easy . . . if it can."

"Fine," the woman said. "You got twenty dollars, I'll
wrap this up for you and make you the gris-gris to wear.
It's a good idea to protect yourself while you're doin' all
this."

Twenty dollars! Laurie had that much money with her,
and more, but what her parents had given her was supposed to be her spending money for the entire time she
was in New Orleans, and she'd been here less than three
days. She took a deep breath and said, "I can't give you
twenty. Will you take ten?"

"Fifteen?"

"Ten and the rest of my goofer dust."

"Okay," the woman said. She took the scarf from Laurie, and soon Laurie had a small bundle to carry and a
gris-gris bag, which the woman tied on a string and insisted that Laurie wear around her neck, tucked under
her shirt.

In spite of the heat Laurie strode as fast as she could to
the streetcar stop and headed for Vivienne's home.

*Vivienne went too far. It's her fault, not mine. Look at her
lying at the foot of the stairs. The fall might have killed her.
Maybe it did. If it didn't, I'll look for the next chance and push
her again.*

*Who does she think she is, sashaying in with that "my" house,
"my" skeleton, and making all those hateful remarks about me?
She says I'm evil. Well, she's right about that. Evil is what I*

wanted to be. The bad voodoo was always more exciting than the good. Phillipe knew all about the evil. He said it was why he had to kill me. That surprised me. I never thought he'd have so much courage.

That girl—Laurie. I suspect she has courage, and that's a worry. The goofer dust she brought to the house—does she know its power? I think so. And how much else does she know about voodoo? It might be dangerous to wait and find out.

She's coming in the back door now, into the kitchen. There are knives in the kitchen. Big, long knives hanging over the stove. People can have fatal accidents with knives.

Laurie's fingers trembled so violently, it was difficult to put the lumps of brimstone on the plate, pour the oily liquid over them, and light the match.

She could feel the evil coming toward her as if it were a low, dark cloud cutting across the sun. The knives on the wall began to rattle as though they, too, were shaking with terror; but Laurie managed to turn from the kitchen counter, shove the plate of burning brimstone toward the horror, and shout, "Evil one, be gone with you! Join your skeleton in the cemetery! Get out of this house! Now!"

A hideous scream raked the kitchen like claws on a windowpane. The glassware in the cupboards trembled, and the walls surged in and out as though they were gasping for breath. Laurie fought to remain on her feet and struggled to keep from dropping the plate of brimstone.

The sulfur stunk as the smoke from it swirled before her face. She choked and coughed, and tears ran from her eyes so she was unable to see, but she kept yelling, "Be gone with you! Join your skeleton in the cemetery! There's a tomb waiting for you!"

"No! This is my *house! Mine!"*

Was it a whisper? A cry? Had she heard the voice only

in her imagination? Laurie didn't wa[...] she could she shouted, "The tomb is y[...] to your tomb and stay there!"

A sudden puff of flame shot through t[...] then died, the terror subsiding with it. [...] that the room was still, and there was n[...] hear her.

She dumped the plate upside down in t[...] threw open a window to get the horrible sme[...] room. The house seemed to breathe and se[...] sigh, as though an invisible peace had lightene[...]

Vivienne called from the living room, [...] Ohhhh! Where are you?"

Laurie ran toward the sound of Vivienne's voic[...] ping short as she saw her grandaunt sprawled o[...] floor. "I'll call an ambulance!" she said.

"No!" Vivienne ordered. "I don't need an an[...] lance."

Laurie glanced at the stairs, at the heel of a sh[...] caught in the carpet halfway down from the landing[...] "Are you sure you don't want a doctor to examine you?"[...] she asked. "That must have been a terrible fall."

"I didn't fall! That horrible ghost pushed me!" Vivienne cried. She sat up and glared at Laurie.

Laurie settled herself cross-legged on the floor facing Vivienne. "You won't have to worry about the ghost any longer," she said. "She's gone, and she won't be back."

Vivienne pursed her lips, and a few wrinkles creased the thick makeup on her forehead. "What nonsense are you talking about?"

"I'm talking about voodoo," Laurie said calmly. "I used brimstone and gris-gris to send the ghost away."

Vivienne's eyes were huge. "Where did you send it?"

"To her tomb in the graveyard."

JOAN LOWERY NIXON

Since she started her writing career in the early sixties, Joan Lowery Nixon has become one of the premier mystery writers for young adults. She is the only author to have won three Edgar Allan Poe awards for Best Juvenile Mystery from Mystery Writers of America, and she is the recipient of many Children's Choice awards throughout the United States. Intertwining dual themes—a personal problem and a mystery to solve—Nixon captures the attention of readers from both angles in her well-known *The Kidnapping of Christina Lattimore, The Ghosts of Now, The Seance, The Other Side of Dark, Whispers from the Dead,* and *Secret, Silent Screams.*

In 1987 she branched off from mysteries to write four books based on the true experiences of orphaned children in the nineteenth century who were sent on trains from New York City to the American Midwest. *A Family Apart, Caught in the Act, In the Face of Danger,* and *A Place to Belong* make up the Orphan Train Quartet. More recently she has provided a look at Hollywood during the past fifty years through a trilogy about one family, called Hollywood Daughters. It includes *Star Baby* (which contains a little of her own young life in that notorious town), *Overnight Sensation,* and *Encore.*

Her newest novels are *A Candidate for Murder* and *High Trail to Danger,* with *The Weekend Was Murder!, A Deadly Promise,* and *Playing for Keeps* scheduled for the near future.

*To Nick, living on an old houseboat on the Nile River in Egypt is
an adventure in itself. Then it gets even more exciting when Nick
discovers the boat has some unexpected residents. . . .*

ANUBIS

ELSA MARSTON

Friday, February 25

It was so peaceful out there on the river tonight, under
the stars, I didn't even notice the smell of old fish. I've
been watching the folks who fish around our houseboat
—actually *living* on their rowboats, whole families
squashed in—and they seem pretty friendly. So when
those two young guys asked if I'd like to go fishing at
night, I was glad to have a chance to hang out with
somebody my own age, even if we couldn't talk much.

I didn't tell Zamaan, though, and was careful not to let
him see me go. With Dad away, Zamaan has been
watching over me as carefully as he has always looked
after the *Isis*—seems like he's been in charge of this boat
for about the last hundred years or so. Sometimes, in fact,
he keeps track of me a little too much . . . like the time
I started to climb up the ladder to the roof and he came
rushing after me, shaking his finger and frowning.
Anyway, he's a good boatman, and with his few words of
English and mine of Arabic, we get along okay. But I
knew he wouldn't have liked my going out with those
fishermen.

We went up the river past the big cruise and restaurant boats. Kamal rowed and Ahmed stood on the back part of the rowboat, letting out the net and pulling it in. Caught five fish, which made him very happy. Close to midnight we finally turned back. Then things changed.

Getting close to the *Isis,* suddenly Kamal stopped rowing. He and Ahmed stared at the dumpy old houseboat I've been living on. There was nothing to see.

But I *felt* something. Waves of tension, almost tangible. Hard to describe . . . maybe like a fever in the boat, or something struggling to fight its way out. For a weird, frightening moment the vibrations seemed to paralyze all three of us.

Then Kamal let his oars drop with a splash and started rowing for dear life—away from the *Isis.* The two of them talked worriedly together in low, guttural voices. I caught one word: *afreet,* evil spirit. Well, whatever . . . there was *something* strange about the boat.

"You want to stay with us?" Kamal offered in Arabic.

Spend the night in a rowboat? I wasn't quite up to that, thanks. So I declined, and Kamal, with a troubled frown on his face, let me off at the dock of a large restaurant boat near the bridge, where I could walk back to my own boat.

Before I left them, Ahmed said in Arabic, "Another time maybe you come with us." But I wonder if they'll ever ask me again. Not likely if I live on a boat full of *afreets*!

Now I'm back on the boat, and it seems to be holding together all right. In fact up till now I've pretty much liked living here. Other people seem to think it's special. A houseboat on the Nile? Man, that's cool!

And in many ways it has been. The wide, green river, palm trees, and the tall minarets of a mosque on the other side, swallows and egrets flying low, and at night the yellow lights on the bridge and the full moon shining on the water . . . it can be really nice. As for cool, if there's a breath of wind, we catch it.

Granted, the boat isn't exactly steady. It does move around and shake you up a bit, and I've cut myself a couple of times shaving. In a strong wind or when a big wake hits, you get a real jolt as the boat pushes against the logs that fend it away from the concrete wall. Sometimes in fact . . . I feel like the boat is reminding me it can't just be taken for granted, like a house or an apartment. It has a life of its own, with its own past and its own personality. And maybe its own intentions.

I wonder what my life in Cairo would have been like if my father had taken an apartment in Maadi, close to the American school and other American kids. But let's face it, I'm kind of a loner; nobody yet has begged me to hang around with them after school. I figured that's how it would be, coming to a new school in January.

So I didn't kick too much when Dad, after a couple of weeks in Egypt, wrote home saying we had the chance to live on a boat in the center of Cairo. It belongs to an American archaeological organization, whose director is an old friend of Dad's, and he's letting us have it for not much rent. They call it the *Isis* after the ancient Egyptian mother-goddess, and it's pretty ancient itself. The blue and white paint job is peeling, the two decks sort of sag, and it lists enough to make doors swing open at odd moments. In the past, archaeologists used to chug up the river in it and live on board, but now, with no motor, it sits permanently moored—for parties and that sort of thing.

I guess the director figured a family would help keep

the boat shipshape. Even a family like ours, w]
has dwindled to one high school junior.

My sister, Lisa, has dropped out of her university in u..
States to find herself. Mom's two months here were like a
tornado, so she went back again to take care of her
career, she said, and Lisa. Then Dad packed up his
computer, put his research on hold, and went home to
see what he could do about pulling the family together.
Promised he'd be back in two weeks, three at most. You'll
manage, Nick, he said; Zamaan will look after you. The
boat's all yours, don't make too-big waves.

Well, we'll see who makes the waves, the boat or me.

It's nearly two now, but I can't sleep. I'm writing this
down because I have a feeling . . . well, what? Maybe
just a feeling I'll want to know what happened. And no,
Zamaan sure wasn't very happy when I came back so late.

Saturday, February 26

This morning was warm and clear, and I couldn't
believe there'd been anything strange about the *Isis* last
night. Especially sitting in a huge, swank apartment high
over the Nile. And how did I get *there*?

So far as I know, Amani Woodberry is the only other
kid at the American high school who lives in this part of
Cairo—in fact just down the street a bit. When she found
out, in history class, that we were taking separate taxis to
school every morning—which sounds crazy but it's
cheaper than the school bus—she thought we should
split a taxi, so to speak. Her parents wanted to meet me,
naturally, so I went to their place this morni
guess I passed. It's worth a try; it'll save my fa
dough.

After we'd settled that, Amani happened

newspaper lying on the coffee table. "Oh, here's that thing our history teacher read us, Nick," she said, picking it up. "Yesterday's *Egyptian Gazette,* where they print juicy news items from the past. The *Gazette*'s more than a hundred years old, you know—naturally the Brits had to have a paper as soon as they took over. Listen to this, folks." Amani is a bit fanatical about Egyptian history, I suppose because her mother is Egyptian.

She started reading. " 'February twenty-fifth, a hundred years ago today. A duly constituted British court of inquiry has completely exonerated Major Kendall Galway of any blame in the recent incident in which a felucca sailboat, overladen with natives, struck the British cruise steamer *Anubis,* with some loss of life. Major Galway admitted to being in the steering house at the time, but only to caution the captain. As Major Galway's legal counsel observed, "It would be unthinkable for a brilliant military career to be tarnished by implication in an incident of so little consequence." ' " Amani slapped the paper down. "I think that's awful!"

Her father said, "What's so awful?"

She snorted. "Don't you *see*? It just shows how callous they were toward the poor Egyptians. Those two guys were probably having a great old time getting sloshed up in the steering house and didn't even *notice* the felucca— with its huge, enormous sail. Oh, well, just blow the natives out of the water if they get in the way."

"Now, Amani," said her mother, "calm down."

So we dropped it. But later, waiting with me for the elevator, Amani said, "Anyway, I'd still like to know how that accident happened. And I hope *somebody* paid for drowning all those poor peasants, don't you?" Her dark eyes, which make her look like she's just stepped down ⁻om an ancient Egyptian tomb painting, shot a challenge at me. Somehow, I bet I haven't heard the last of that ill-fated felucca.

And I heard a lot more today than just that. I *think*.

Halfway through the evening I was trying to do my algebra in the lounge when, with a soft squeak, the door swung half open. I thought it was Zamaan, maybe bringing me a cup of tea, all spiffed up in the clean galabia gown he puts on at suppertime. He's a strange man, tall and stiff and sort of proper—not like most Egyptians, who are so easygoing and chatty. Lean, dark face and surprising eyes, a real clear blue. Hard to guess his age; sometimes looks younger than my father—other times pretty old. Never smiles. Can't say I feel very easy with him, but I respect him.

Anyway, this time no Zamaan appeared.

My second thought was the way the boat lists, so sometimes an unlatched door on one side will swing open. Then it dawned on me, the door was on the *other* side. There was no wind, no heavy wake from a passing barge, no way that door could swing open by itself. I got up and pulled it shut, shivering in the evening breeze.

But hold it. I just said it was a calm night, didn't I? And it was. Yet I know I felt a breath of cold air, and it chilled me to my bones.

Well, anything can happen, living on the river. I tried to get back to my homework. But before long I began to be aware of something. The room, with its pictures of ancient Egyptian gods on the walls, was strangely noisy. I don't mean sound, exactly, but . . . somehow, a voice.

Gradually words took shape, phrases with a British accent, a woman's voice, quiet and very refined-sounding, but with a lot going on underneath. First I tried to shut it out, because I couldn't believe in it. Then I had to listen.

"*. . . it suits him, yes, just beautifully . . .*" I heard. "*. . . the master . . . the noble calling . . . and it is only right, so he informs me, that others make their sacrifices too. . . .*"

I looked around, utterly bewildered. What was *that* all about?

Then: "*Ah!* My *happiness! That concerns him?*" Silence, and a light musical clink. Like a teacup set down in a saucer.

The voice—or the shadow of a voice—went on. "*Yes, of course you would speak of duty, Angelica, his duty to discipline this disorderly little corner of the world, mine to remain at his side. . . .*"

A sigh, another little clink of china, and nothing more. A night bird squawked mournfully, and I shivered again, feeling more alone than ever. Then I pushed the algebra aside and started to write.

Sunday, February 27

Slow morning. No job, no buddies to go riding with at the Pyramids or poking around the bazaar shops at Khan el Khalili. I stood on the newly varnished deck, leaning on the rail as I gazed at the sunlight on the river, and wondered what folks would think if I said I heard teacups and voices in the middle of my algebra last night. Were they really there? Or . . . only in my head?

Had to do *something* to get off this boat! I thought of Amani and her babbling about that antique news item. And I had an idea.

Phoned her—yes, I actually phoned her! And she answered.

I started out really suave. "Just wondering—like what if we tried to find out more about that old accident, you know, the cruise boat and the felucca? We could maybe write a history paper on—on something. I mean, there's sort of a personal connection, me living on a boat. Think the *Gazette* office might still have those old issues?"

"Nick, that sounds like fun!" she said, and I nearly fell overboard. "I'd love to mess around in some hundred-year-old dirt. Let's go!"

The taxi found the *Gazette* building on a narrow, noisy street in downtown Cairo. We marched in, climbed several dingy flights of stairs, and ricocheted from one frantic office to another until we ended up in a little back room filled with huge folios of crumbling yellowed paper. And they still had some of the really early issues! It took plenty of patience, turning those pages.

We started with February 25th, of course, the date when that British major got off. Not a word about it. Slowly we went back almost three months, looking for something about the investigation. Nothing. At last, about to chuck the whole thing, I had another bright idea.

"Could the *Gazette* have messed up the date?"

"Never," Amani said with heavy sarcasm. "But just on the very remote chance, let's move forward."

And there, March 3rd, we found it. The report of the incident itself, on February 29th. It wasn't just "some loss of life," as the other account had put it. All but two peasants, out of more than forty, had drowned when their ferry was cut in half by the *Anubis*. On her maiden voyage yet. Some question as to who was at the wheel and why the felucca was not avoided.

"I knew it!" said Amani. "Both of those guys up in the steering house totally smashed!" She likes to make a good story, it seems.

We went on, through June. Never found the item

picked up by the *Gazette* in our own time. But on the editorial page of June 28th, we found this:

> An unfortunate scene took place at the conclusion of the court hearing at which Mr. Abdul Saeed, captain of the S.S. *Anubis,* was found fully responsible for the sinking of a ferry at Luxor. Mr. Saeed, although an Egyptian, had been employed by the steamship line for several years, giving quite satisfactory service. Yet on being led away, he was heard to utter the following, inexcusably intemperate, remarks: "So, Major Galway, you have your way. And may you be d————d for it! You'll not be free of the *Anubis* if it takes a hundred years to make you pay."

I turned to Amani. "Sounds to me," I said in a tone of mock horror, "like a curse."

She shuddered elaborately and rolled her eyes. "I wouldn't step foot on the S.S. *Anubis* after that."

"Me neither. You wouldn't catch me dead on that tub." We both laughed. But I was wondering. What could have happened to the *Anubis,* anyway, after that scandal?

In the late afternoon, alone again, I sat doing homework in the glassed-in sun deck at the bow. Must confess, in spite of the morning's thrill of sharing dirt, dust, and even lunch with Amani, I was feeling a little down.

So was somebody else.

Very soft, like a ripple against the boat, I heard a sigh . . . and then a sob.

I couldn't help looking around me, though I knew I was alone in a room filled with sunlight. Caught a whiff of jasmine and noticed a vase of flowers behind me. I got up to smell them. Totally withered. Probably been there since the time when Mom was here.

And then that sad voice again! *"Oh, darling, it's*

you . . . *yes, of course, quite all right. No, it's just a little—
a little bit of sand in my eye . . . the* khamsin *winds . . . yes, I
know that, darling, and I am trying, truly I am . . . it's just
the* khamsin. . . ."

Could it be, I wondered, an echo of my mother? But
Mom's voice had definitely not been sad or gentle! Then
who? A thought hit me. If some strong emotion or conflict between people was expressed in a room, could it
somehow permeate the very walls—and maybe linger on
for years and years?

No, I thought, that's just fiction, and this is just my
nerves. After all, I'm only seventeen, left on my own in a
strange land—I've a perfect right to hear things! And I
know about the *khamsin*. It makes you damned edgy, that
wind, thick and yellow with fine sand from the desert,
blowing and blowing like it's trying to get into your very
mind.

But there was no *khamsin* this afternoon. The air was
like a spring day at home.

Now, tonight, the boat is acting up. I can't believe the
way it rocks and shakes, jolts and jars and jerks, shoving
me all over the place! In the kitchen I slopped my lentil
soup all over. And when I got down to clean up the floor,
the fridge door swung open and walloped me. I yelled,
wanted somebody to yell at, or to comfort me, or anything. Somebody solid, I mean.

My 7UP tipped over on my econ book, water drips nonstop from the bathtub faucet like the pipes have gone
bonkers, and the floor sort of pushes me around when I
try to cross the room. Suddenly, out of the corner of my
eye, I see somebody move in the bathroom, a tall, thin
form, and my heart thunks. Then I realize it's only the
shower curtain swishing back and forth.

And outside, those logs keep thumping against the

wall. I feel the thud in my guts—unh! unh! unh!—deep
and persistent as pain. But when I go out on the deck, I
don't see furrows in the dark water or hear any rhythmic
sloshing of a wake. There's not a whiff of wind, the water
is completely calm.

Yet the boat keeps straining, like a chained animal
struggling to get free.

Monday, February 28

I woke early and heard voices close by the boat. Maybe
fishermen, I thought. Then I recalled I hadn't seen
Kamal and Ahmed since that night, and the other boats
aren't coming near the *Isis* anymore. Are they afraid?

The voices *were* fishermen, though: on shore, helping
with one of the logs. It had cracked, and it looked like
any more pressure would break it in two. Zamaan,
looking worried and tired, directed them from the boat. I
couldn't help noticing the fishermen's faces, their scared
eyes. They hurried clumsily, like they wanted to get away
as fast as they could.

And something else this morning. A new man has
come to work on the boat—sent by the archaeological
outfit that owns it, I guess, to help Zamaan. Can't think of
any other reason he'd turn up. His name is Sayid. Hard
to tell his age, like Zamaan. But a much more typical
Egyptian, as laid-back and friendly as Zamaan is aloof.
Big, good-natured smile. I don't know how Zamaan feels
about him, though; he sure didn't look very happy.
Maybe because Sayid wasn't lifting a finger to help with
the log problem.

I met Amani and the taxi but didn't tell her about the
boat or the things I was hearing. Man, I wish I could tell
somebody . . . especially her. That morning at the

Gazette was the most fun I've had since coming here. But would the story get around school that Nick Tempe thinks the old boat he lives on is haunted? That would go over just great.

When I got home from school, Zamaan met me on the gangplank. Sayid was standing behind him on the deck, not quite smiling this time, and I wondered how their day together had gone. It seemed to me Zamaan looked a lot older, gray and exhausted, his blue eyes cloudy, like he'd aged years in just the last couple of days.

"Broken," he said, pointing to the electric cable that runs from the boat to some mysterious hookup on shore. Then he made his way down the narrow side deck to the stern, beckoning to me to follow. I walked along the little garden between the river wall and the stone-paved bank below the street level. He pointed to the spot where an iron link chain, one of the two that moor the *Isis* to land, is fastened to something set in the concrete. The chain had pulled partway loose. That's all we need, I thought— the whole boat breaking away! Worried, I turned back to check on the other chain.

But a quick glance at the stern of the boat stopped me. The sunlight was reflecting strangely off the water, flickering over the blunt rear end. And there I saw something I hadn't noticed before.

Something had apparently been glued or nailed onto the stern in the past, leaving a sort of faint patch in the white paint. As I stared at it, the blob seemed to take shape. A dog, crouching with its paws outstretched, a dog with a long, sharp muzzle and large, pricked ears.

I tried to think why that image looked familiar. Then, with a shot of apprehension, I hurried back to the gangplank. Sayid was standing there, half smiling, but I just pushed past him and ran up the narrow, steep stairs to the upper deck. In the lounge, among the other framed prints of the old gods, I saw the same image.

Anubis, jackal god of ancient Egypt, guardian of the dead.

So the *Isis* had started out with a very different personality! Anubis! But . . . No. I pushed aside the next thought. No, it wasn't possible. A small, ordinary cruise steamer just wouldn't last that long. There was no way that our boat could be the very same *Anubis* as the one in the accident a hundred years ago. Or . . . could it? What about those feverish vibrations, that unhappy voice, the weird fury of the boat? All these thoughts seemed to turn my head to face the picture of the jackal god again. And as the scary truth crept through me, I felt my insides turn to slush.

I went out on the deck to pace back and forth, trying to deal with this, shivering with clammy sweat in the cool afternoon breeze. Things like this just couldn't happen!

Suddenly I jumped, startled. A violent sound—the crack of a rifle! Nearly lost my balance, wobbly with panic. Then, whew! I thought, a car backfires and I think somebody's shooting. All the old rattletraps still on the streets—

And I heard the voice again.

"He's up there—Angelica, he's up there again, practicing his marksmanship, he says . . . wild fowl, the peasants' pigeons, cats, and someday, when . . . when he is not seeing quite clearly . . . perhaps a child. A dirty little native child, whom nobody would miss. . . ."

The voice broke, and if there were any more words, the wind blew them away. I sat on the top step, head in my hands, for a long time. Now I know what happened to the *Anubis*. It's alive—but not well. And I'm on it.

* * *

The night is fierce, for Cairo. In the light from the cafés I see whitecaps on the river, big ones, and the black troughs of advancing waves.

Spasm after spasm grips the boat, and the dry wood whimpers. Once when I got up, the floor seemed to pull away from under me, and I fell hard against the wooden table. The doors vibrate and fly open, then crash shut again. Everything rattles that *can* rattle—sliding windows, saucepans, the gods on the walls. The whole boat shivers and twitches so much, I can hardly write this!

Suddenly I think of the way a dog shakes itself to throw water off its coat. Anubis is, after all, a kind of dog.

Rhythmic drumbeats come across the water from a café where people are having a good time, and I think, *Why do I have to deal with this by myself?* I feel rocked with anger at my parents, at my self-seeking sister. I'm not used to managing things. Other people have always done it. Now all of a sudden I'm on my own—which is enough, if you ask me—and everything goes crazy in the only home I've got, for now.

Thank God, at least there's Zamaan. He knows how to take care of things.

Wait, let me think. About Zamaan. This is the only home *he's* got. The only place he's lived for a long, long time, so far as I know. I can always go back to the U.S. if I have to, and Smilin' Sayid doesn't have to stay either; but where would Zamaan go? He doesn't seem to have any family—I don't think he's ever even had a friend come to see him. And he really loves the old boat. Keeps the brass fittings polished, decks swabbed—in fact, come to think of it, I've never seen him *off* the boat. Working by day, pacing on the deck at night . . . a strange and lonely life, but I guess it's all he's got.

Anyway I've made up my mind. The boat may be coming apart, but I won't desert it. No rat, I. For Zamaan's sake—and in a way I can't quite explain, for *mine*—I'll stay on board. Whatever is bewitching this boat —whatever drove away my mother and then my father and now may be trying to get rid of me—I'll face it.

I hear a street dog barking, then a long, desolate howl —and I remember something. Every stray dog in Cairo, every last one, has the long, thin muzzle, the scrawny flanks, the pointed ears . . . of the jackal.

And later . . .

Things happened fast, that last night—February 29th. An awful *khamsin* blew all day. When I got home from school, I saw the boat's chain almost yanked out of the retaining wall. The other one had nearly pulled over the mango tree it was fastened to. Zamaan shuffled about on the boat, doing whatever he could, though he looked really frazzled. Sayid smiled at me, but I could see he wasn't helping much. Those two obviously didn't work together well, and I was afraid it would be bad if things got really out of control.

In the evening, the wind still blowing hard and air thick with dust, the boat heaved and jerked like a living thing. I felt so helpless and alone, couldn't concentrate, couldn't do anything useful, just pace around, agitated. On impulse I picked up the phone. Heard the dial tone —unbelievable! The thing still worked!

Amani answered, and everything went out of my head. What did I want to tell her anyway?

"Well," I stammered, "just thought I'd—how're things?"

She sounded surprised. "Fine here, bit gritty is all. Hey, Nick? Nick? What's—"

The phone went dead. I slammed the receiver down, then thought, *It's just as well. No way Amani could help.*

But a few minutes later as I looked out the window, there she was! She came hurrying down the long flight of steps from the street, dodging the branches of the rubber trees, and, watching, I didn't know whether I wanted her with me or a hundred miles away. I stumbled down the stairway to the lower deck, knocked from side to side by the wild rolling of the boat.

"Wait!" I yelled as Amani approached the gangplank, which was now twisted to a grotesque angle. Clutching at the wooden rail, I lurched across and nearly fell off the other end onto dry land.

"Hi, Nick, wow—this wind!" Amani yelped as she tried to hold her scarf on. "Listen, anything wrong? You sounded—"

"Amani, you'd better get out of here!"

"Well, what's that supposed to mean? Nick, I know something's bothering you, I've felt it the last couple of days. A letter from your folks, maybe? Look, let me come on board and we'll just talk for a while. You know," she added with a forced little smile, "I've never been on your boat—"

A sharp crack cut her off. The log had taken about all the battering it could. Another minute and the boat might be crushed against the concrete wall.

"Get away, Amani!" I shouted. "The boat's—not fun at all!"

Her eyes filled with anger and disappointment. "I'm just trying to help, dammit!"

Suddenly a cry came from the lower deck. I spun around and saw Zamaan at the other end of the gangplank. He made a frantic gesture, repeating a phrase I couldn't understand. Was he telling me to stay off?

But the boat was in danger—and Zamaan himself. No sign of Sayid. He'd probably quit, jumped ship, him and his big, friendly smile. I couldn't think straight. But it seemed to me the least I could do, if the boat was determined to wreck itself, was help Zamaan. Even if he didn't want me to.

My legs nearly buckling, I started back across the gangplank. It swayed and jounced like a rope bridge over a canyon. The cords that fastened the thing in place were pulling looser and looser.

"Nick! I'm coming too!"

Amani's cry reached me as I landed on the deck. Already halfway across the gangplank, she staggered along a few more steps—and the cords pulled apart. Just as the gangplank broke away, she leaped. I caught her, and we both sprawled on the narrow deck, bumping heads and knees.

Again there was a strangled shout from Zamaan. But where was he? He'd always stood ready—and now when he was really needed, he had disappeared!

"This is crazy!" gasped Amani.

In the bow of the boat I caught a glimpse of Zamaan's galabia whipping in the wind as he slipped around the corner out of sight. I pushed Amani toward the lower-deck lounge, shouting, "Stay here, it's safer—I gotta help Zamaan!" Grabbing the rail as the boat tipped this way and that, I headed for the bow.

"No—you're not going up there again!"

She hadn't even listened to me! Ticked off at her, I paused—and then realized what I'd heard. *Again?* I'd never gone "up there" at all! I turned and, from the look on Amani's face, I knew she hadn't even spoken.

"Please . . . darling, listen to me . . . it isn't right . . . !"
The cry was lost in the grit-filled wind.

I felt torn, wanting to ask Amani if she'd heard the voice too. The boat was rocking so badly, though, shoving and straining in all directions, I had to help deal with that first—if I could.

But when I reached the bow, I didn't find Zamaan wrestling with the log or the iron chain. He had disappeared again. Then, once more a flicker of that galabia caught my eye. The old man was climbing the ladder to the steering house on the roof!

He's out of his mind, I thought. Maybe he thinks he can steer if the boat breaks loose. But the steering thing must've gone ages ago!

The thin metal ladder was not fastened at the bottom. Screws had given way, so it hung several inches above the deck. I remembered Zamaan's earlier warning and saw that it might pull loose or break through. I sure didn't want to go up on it—the gangplank had been awful, and this looked even worse.

Amani came stumbling out to the bow. "Nick, for pete's sake—"

"Boatman's up there!" I shouted over the whistling wind. "He'll fall—got to get him down!"

She seemed to understand, didn't say anything more. Just braced herself against the wild heaving of the boat and held the ladder while I started up the thin, rusty bars. Still, it swayed so much, I could hardly pry my hands loose for each step.

At last I reached the top and flung myself onto the narrow walkway of weathered wooden planks. Then, on hands and knees, I crept toward the steering house. It was just a small cabin with windows on three sides, perched on the flat roof of the boat.

But where was Zamaan? Nowhere in sight! Even in the darkness, in the swirling, dust-filled air, he couldn't just disappear. I shouted for him, but heard nothing. Had he fallen off? No, he'd have yelled, there'd have been a big splash. So he must've already gotten inside the steering house. But the door had to be locked—could he have the key?

I inched closer, the cabin's paint flaking off as I tried to cling to the sides and peer through the dirty glass. Flashes of streetlight through the tossing palm branches made it just possible to see the small room.

No one was in there.

And then I heard a voice—from inside the steering house! I slid down below the window and listened, scarcely believing.

"*. . . Yes, little lady thinks she's had enough. . . .*" It was a male voice, heavy British accent. "*. . . says she's not too happy here . . . give her everything. . . . Spoiled, tha's all, wouldn' you say so, m'friend?*"

A light clink, like two glasses together, or a bottle on a rim. Then, "*Well, here's to us, we know how to live, don' we, m' dark and dusky friend. . . . Can't help it if she's bored, can' be with her every minute. . . .*"

The voice ceased, and I huddled there, paralyzed by what I was hearing. And suddenly, like a lightning strike, it hit me. There was only one other presence besides me on the roof. If Zamaan had disappeared and that voice had come, were they—could they possibly be the same?

Still barely grasping the idea, I heard the voice again: "*. . . ferry up ahead. Good God, look at 'em, packed in like pigs. Live like an'mals . . . wonder if they've got the brains to be bored. . . .*"

And then—"*Here, lemme have the wheel. Put a little*

'citement in those mis'rable lives . . . give little lady bit of excitement too. . . . No, no, let me! I can handle it. Ne'er mind the tricky winds—I can handle anything. Jus' see how close we can get. . . ."

Through the bluster of the wind and the dull city roar came a new sound. Distant cries, cries of terror—

And once more the voice: *"Tha's all, lit'le thrill on the ol' Nile—no! NO! Get away—I've got the wheel! GET YOUR BLEEDIN' HANDS OFF!"*

A scream tore through the wind and night. Still crouched by the door, I felt a terrible, shuddering lurch and grabbed for the rusted handle. The boat, pulling free of the chains, swung out into the river. And as it did so, again I seemed to hear the street dogs bark, and an anguished howl rose around me.

Or was it a howl of triumph?

Rolling from one side to the other, the boat turned in a full circle. The wind was blowing downstream now and lashed the water into high, whitecapped waves. Wind and current carried us faster and faster toward the bridge.

I thought of Amani and tried to scream down to her. "Get back! Inside!" But my chest felt almost too tight to breathe, and the words just blew away. Again, as I hung on to the door handle, I tried to peer through the grimy window, desperately hoping there might be something left to steer with.

My blood froze at what I saw.

There *was* a steering wheel—and two figures struggling to seize it. One was Zamaan—and the other, Sayid! They wrestled and strained, but did not make a sound. Not a word, not the slightest thud as they staggered this way and that. And I knew at last they could not be flesh and blood.

Then I glanced toward the front of the boat—and my heart almost stopped. We were plowing, hell-bent, straight at the abutment of the bridge. A square hit, and the old boat would be smashed to pieces!

I must've gone out of my mind right then. All I could do was shake that door, shake it with all my strength. The two specters inside turned toward me, and for a terrifying instant our eyes met. Did they know me? Could they understand that not everybody on that damned boat was ready to die?

With a horrifying shriek of wood and metal the boat hit the bridge. But at the last split second it swerved! Something turned the boat so that it struck at an angle and veered off to one side, then headed for the low metal substructure. Thrown down hard by the sudden swerve, I lay flat on the splintery planks, petrified with fear as the boat swept under the bridge. Beside me the steering house was sheared right off. With a last, blood-chilling groan, it fell into the river.

The *Anubis,* wallowing in circles, one side crushed in, tipped farther and farther. It was sinking. I dragged myself to the edge of the uptilted roof and found I could lower myself to the deck.

But where was Amani? Had she been hurt when the boat struck? I yelled, hardly daring even to hope she was all right.

At the same instant her voice reached me, frantic, but real. "Nick! Where are you? *Nick, are you okay?"* And I knew I was not alone.

As we floundered in the river a few minutes later, making our way to shore, we looked back at the shattered frame of the *Anubis* in the dark waters. Slowly it disintegrated, part sinking, part floating away, until it no longer resembled a boat. With it, I knew—and *only I* knew —went the doomed presence that had been imprisoned on that boat for the last hundred years. Major Galway had paid.

ELSA MARSTON

While much of Elsa Marston's previous writing for young people has been nonfiction—most notably *Mysteries in American Archaeology; Art in Your Home Town; Some Artists, Their Lives, Loves, and Luck;* and *The Lebanese in America*—young adult fiction has always been her favorite type of writing, and she has published one young adult novel: *The Cliffs of Cairo.*

Her lifelong interest in other times and places earned her a master's degree in international affairs at Harvard University, followed by a year at the American University of Beirut, Lebanon. She and her Lebanese husband usually live in Bloomington, Indiana, where he is a professor and she was an instructor for the Institute of Children's Literature, but their professions and interests have provided them with several travel and living experiences overseas in Egypt, Lebanon, Tunisia, and Greece. All of these places have provided Marston with exotic settings for her writing. In fact she wrote "Anubis" in 1991 while living in Cairo on the very boat described in her story. The real boat didn't seem to be haunted, but—she is quick to add—"one never knows."

Her most recent publications are both picture books: one about a young girl who learns how to deal with pirates—*Cynthia and the Runaway Gazebo;* and the other about a boy and a griffin that makes itself a little too much "to home"—*A Griffin in the Garden.*

A powerful and wicked man in life, Thomas Warner is not happy to find himself dead and very lonely. How, he wonders, can he get himself out of this. . . ?

SAVE THE ELEPHANT, THE ANT, AND BILLIKINS

VIVIEN ALCOCK

I could not believe I was dead. It was most extraordinary. I had been lying in bed when—pop! I shot up in the air like a champagne cork. Like in the song—

> *There was an old woman tossed up in a blanket*
> *Seventeen times as high as the moon . . .*

But I am not an old woman. I am a very rich man, I thought, and if the fools I pay to look after me have done this, then they will suffer for it. Just wait till I come down.

But I didn't come down. I remained in the air, bobbing against the ceiling like a helium-filled balloon. Looking down, I could see them bending over my bed. The doctor said, "He's gone."

"I'm not 'gone,' you imbecile! I'm up here!" I shouted.

They ignored me. The doctor was filling up a form. The nurse was bending over the—*There was someone in my bed!* In my bed, in my silk pajamas, with his head on my best goose-feather pillow. With a great effort I managed to sink a few inches from the ceiling. Now I could see clearly who was lying on my bed. It was me!

"No!" I shouted, "It can't be! I'm up here! Don't cover my face, you stupid woman!"

The nurse drew the sheet over my face on the pillow. For a moment everything went white, as blank as snow; then I could see as clearly as before. They were walking toward the door. I heard my housekeeper say, "It's a merciful release." She looked like a cat who is dreaming of the cream pot.

With a sort of furious wiggle, I propelled myself toward her right ear. "I haven't left you a penny in my will, you ugly old bag!" I shouted.

She gave a little shiver and looked over her shoulder. "It's cold in here," she said.

"The chill of death," said the nurse. "I don't know about you. I could do with a nice cup of tea."

"It's *my* tea!" I screamed. "I forbid you to have any! Do you hear me?"

It was obvious that they did not. They all left the room, and I heard them chattering down the stairs. Going to drink my tea, eat my biscuits; the doctor would probably help himself to my whiskey! And there was nothing I could do about it. For the first time, alone in my room with my sheeted corpse below me, I realized I was dead.

And I was frightened.

"God forgive me," I whispered, for I had been a wicked man.

All that night I cowered in the dark room. Waiting for something to happen. Waiting in terror for an avenging angel or grinning devil to fetch me away.

After three months I would have welcomed them. Better Hell than this. For three empty months I drifted around my house, unnoticed, unmourned. Sometimes I wept, though no tears fell. Sometimes I cursed and shouted defiance. No one heard me. You can't imagine what it was like—how cold, how terrible.

People came to the house, the undertakers, the lawyer, my shabby nephew and his thin wife. I fluttered around them, like a moth drawn to bright candles.

"Listen to me! Speak to me! Forgive me!" I wept. "For pity's sake, speak to me."

My nephew shivered. His wife turned up her coat collar. The others paid me no attention at all. They ignored me. *Me!* I was—had been—a powerful man. A hard man fighting my way out of the slum where I was born. "I'm a self-made man," I had often boasted. But now that manufactured man was dead and buried. I was once again a small child crying for love.

It was odd. I could see and hear. I could move about at will, though I had no feet to run with, nor hands to push myself along. I swam through the air like a tadpole through water. I went through doors like a worm through mud. I could go anywhere I wanted—but there was nowhere I wanted to go.

The house was shut up. Occasionally a house agent brought around prospective buyers. They looked around. They shivered and asked if the house was damp. Nobody heard me. Nobody saw me. I was only a slight chill in the air. No more than that.

"God forgive me, punish me, send me to Hell," I pleaded, "only don't leave me all alone."

After a year I pulled myself together. "Use your brain, Thomas Warner," I said (not that I had one, but old habits of speech died hard). "You are a ghost. Now, what do I know about ghosts? Let me see. They haunt the place where they were murdered. . . . But I wasn't murdered. I drove my car into a tree when I was drunk and died in my own bed. What else? They are condemned to stay on earth until they have righted the wrongs they have done—''

If I'd had a heart, it would have sunk to the floor. How could I possibly right all the wrongs I had done? There were hundreds of people I had cheated on my way to the top. I couldn't even remember their names.

I went out into the garden. I could no longer bear the empty house. All night I wailed with the wind, wept with the rain. It was me you heard beating against your window. It was me you heard moaning at your door. But none of you let me in.

The morning came cold and clear, with a pale sun in the washed sky. I knew then what I must do. I must search the world to find someone I could reach, even if it took a thousand years. I must tell them where my gold lay buried and beg them to give it to charity. I must buy a ticket to Heaven. There must be someone, somewhere, who could see me.

I found her that afternoon, in a garden not three miles away from my home. She was sitting on a lawn in the sun, reading a book. I looked over the hedge at her without much hope. She was a girl of about fourteen or fifteen, with improbable apricot-colored hair. Her face was flushed, and she sniffed now and then, as if she had a cold or had been crying. She was dressed in the gear they all wear: faded blue denim trousers and a sweatshirt with writing on it—SAVE THE ELEPHANT AND THE ANT. Ridiculous.

I have always disliked teenagers. There is something about them that makes me want to scratch. They wear

efer the taxman t

to say *"After* you've

by cats, ginger cats,
the sun, stalking in
aling from dustbins.

ard me. Whiskered
ey saw me and they

d the cats watched

ver the garden of a
ugh the weeds and
ewing.

ground. Brambles
tickling sensation.
ying on the ground
. I peered into the
o yellow eyes like

t? I had no hands. I
back to the girl and

hen I heard a voice
nd?"

in a neat gray suit.

silly clothes and giggle. They rush about on noisy motorbikes, getting in the way of my car. One moment they're drooping around the town with their arms around each other as if in need of support. The next they're sheer energy, running down the quiet streets of my suburb, leaping up to pluck leaves off the overhanging trees. *My* trees. *My* leaves.

Worst of all, they have no respect for money. Oh, they like spending it, as any parents will tell you, but they're just as likely to give it away to their friends, or to some lost cause—"Save the Elephant and the Ant." That's typical. Who cares about the elephant and the ant? They do. That's the trouble with them. They think the world's worth saving.

I would have passed her by, but at that moment she looked up and said, "Go away!"

"You can see me!" I cried with delight. "You can see me!"

"Go away!" she said again, and blew her nose on a grubby handkerchief.

I stayed where I was, hovering above the hedge, not wanting to go nearer in case she retreated to the house.

"May I talk to you?" I asked humbly. "Don't be afraid. I won't hurt you. I just want to ask you something."

"No."

"Why not?"

"I'm not allowed to talk to ghosts," she told me. "Dad says it's freaky, and Ma says it'll put people off me. She means boys of course. She's wrong, but it's no good telling her. So you'd better go away."

"Do you always do what your mother says?" I asked, hoping to shame her into rebellion.

She shrugged and muttered, "It's boring talking to ghosts. They're always moaning about something."

If I'd had a hand, I'd have slapped
wonder if I'll ever learn to be good.

We sat in silence. At least, she sat on
floated about two inches above the hedg
at her. There was a small hole in her swe
denim trousers were frayed, and her hair
ing bush. She didn't look like a girl who h
her appearance, but you couldn't always t
it amuses them to go around in rags.

Then I noticed the silver bracelets on
There must have been over a dozen of th
cheap enough, some of them bent out of s

"If you do me a small favor," I said, "you
gold bracelet."

"Don't like gold," she said.

Didn't like gold! What can you do with a
that? I suppose the color doesn't match her e

I kept my temper. "You can buy things wit
pointed out patiently, "whatever you like. Or
give it to charity, if that's what you go for. You m
be able to save the green-spotted bog beetle."

She laughed at that. She looked very pretty
laughed.

"You made that up," she said. "There's no su
ture."

She wasn't stupid. I was glad she had a sense of
I almost liked her. It was an odd feeling, a sort of
I'd never felt before, not even when I was as young
was.

"Is there anything you want?" I asked gently.

The laughter left her face.

"I want Billy," she said. "I want Billikins back."

Who could be worth more than gold to her?

"Your boyfriend? Your brother?" I asked.

"The taxman," I said. "Do you p
your cat?"

"No."

"So you'll do it?"

I was glad to see she had the sense
got me Billikins back."

Oh, that suburb was full of cats: ta
black cats, and tortoiseshell. Lying in
the long grass, climbing up trees, ste
But no Billikins.

I called his name and the cats he
heads turned, yellow eyes glared. Th
spat.

"Billikins! Billikins!" I shouted, a
me and growled in their throats.

I nearly missed him. I was drifting
large, old house, peering down thr
the brambles, when I heard a faint

"Billikins?"

"Meow!"

Where was he? I sank toward th
dragged through me with an odd
Then I saw the well. The cover was
beside it, the wood half rotted awa
dark hole and saw, far below, tw
drowned suns staring up at me.

Billikins. How was I to get him ou
couldn't even lift a feather. I must go
tell her where her cat was.

I was about to leave the garden w
say, "What can I do for you, my frie
I turned and saw a gray-haired ma
"You can see me!" I cried.

"I can indeed," he said, smiling. "I'm a sensitive. Nicholas Fry, at your service. Always glad to help the dear departed. Why have you come to me? Is it a message for a loved one?"

I looked at him. I doubt if I would have trusted him when I was alive, but then I had trusted no one. And it was either him or the teenage girl. My instincts were against the girl. She was young, with a head stuffed full of dreams and ideals, and all her mistakes still to be made.

On the other hand the man looked sharp enough, in spite of the nonsense about the "dear departed." He'd be willing to help me for a fee, with none of the trouble of rescuing a cat. I didn't need the girl now.

"I have a proposition to put to you," I said.

I told him about my buried gold. I offered him a quarter share to keep for himself. I saw his eyes widen.

"Very generous," he said.

"I want the rest to go to charity."

"Charity, eh? Very nice. That's what I like, someone with a kind heart," he said, rubbing his hands together. "Any particular charity in mind?"

I thought of the girl and said, "A charity that rescues endangered species."

He nodded his head. "I see, sir. Very nice. Save the whale, that sort of thing? Elephants, sir? Right you are. I'll do that for you. Where is this gold of yours, then?"

"Just a minute," I said.

I don't know why I didn't tell him and have done with it. I had to trust someone. Why did I keep thinking of the girl? I saw her laughing over the green-spotted bog beetle. I remembered how she'd looked sorry for me. She had wanted to help me, I knew that. It was not only her cat. She had wanted to save the elephant and the ant *and* the ghost too.

"There's a cat down your well," I said.

He wasn't interested. "Wretched creatures. Always getting in where they shouldn't. It can stay there. The well's dry. It won't come to any harm."

"It will starve. I want you to bring it out."

He gave in immediately, smiling and saying, "Now, that's kind. An animal lover, are we, sir? That's what I like to see."

Then he fetched a basket and a rope from the house, and he let it down the well. The little cat cowered away from the basket and spat. The man said something under his breath.

"I'll entice him into the basket," I said. "Wait here."

The bottom of the well was choked with dead leaves and rubbish. Water gleamed through the latticework of twigs on which the cat crouched. He was shivering, and his eyes watched me as I floated down. He liked me even less than he liked the basket. He spat and his claws raked through me.

I laughed. So small and full of courage. His fur was spiky, his legs thin as needles, and his sides concave, but what brave defiance blazed in his eyes.

I darted toward him, and he lashed out again. His paw went right through me, and he fell on his nose. Around and around we went as I tried to chase him into the basket.

"Hurry up!" the old man called.

I was—or had been—an obstinate man. I was not going to give up. I liked the brave little cat. I hovered above his head. He leaped up, trying to catch me, and missed. Now I danced around him like a demented fly, and he sprang after me, scrabbling at the wall, bouncing off the twigs, leaping over the basket. His eyes were gleaming, and I heard a loud rattle coming from his throat. He was purring. It was a game now. I had found a playmate at last.

"You're wasting time!" the man shouted.

I whizzed past the cat's nose and darted into the bucket. He sprang in after me, and the old man began to pull us up. I could feel the little cat's heart beating with terror as the basket swayed and bumped against the walls.

"It's all right," I whispered, "you're safe."

He looked at me with huge yellow eyes. Perhaps he understood, for he did not move. Then we were out in the air. The old man grabbed Billikins roughly by the scruff of his neck and dumped him on the ground. The cat streaked away without a backward glance. I hoped he knew his way home.

"Now, what about our agreement?" the old man asked.

I told him where I had hidden my gold. In which garden, beneath which tree, how far down. As I spoke, I saw an expression I knew only too well come into his face, an expression I had seen in my own mirror. Greed.

"You can keep half!" I cried wildly. "The rest is for charity, remember?"

He smiled and rubbed his hands together. I had thought I could trust him. How could I have been so horribly mistaken? His little eyes glinted redly, as if lit by sparks of fire. His smile vanished into folds of fat. He began to laugh until the earth shook. I backed away from him. He was evil, a devil. I had gambled and I had lost. I'd have done far better to have trusted a child.

I let the wind blow me where it would. Down little streets I whirled, with the dead leaves and the rubbish. Litter, that's all I was, discarded, unwanted. I must have gone around in circles, because at last I came to a hedge I recognized. It was night now. Her forgotten book lay on the moonlit lawn. I wondered if Billikins had got home safely.

Then I saw him, stepping daintily over the grass toward me. His eyes were brighter than sovereigns. His whiskers smelled of cream.

"Hullo, Billikins," I said.

He blinked at me in greeting and twitched his tail like a finger beckoning. Then he ran off.

I followed him. He seemed to know where he was going, running swiftly and silently, his black fur silvered by the moonlight. He led me to an open square, then stopped, sat down, and began to wash his paws.

"Funny sort of angel you've got," said a voice.

I was no longer alone. Suddenly the night was crowded with beings like myself. Ghosts, I suppose you would call them. To me they were what I'd wanted and never had. Friends.

"Glad you got here in the end."

"Thought you'd never make it."

"We've been waiting ages."

I looked up gratefully at the sky. The night was bright with stars.

VIVIEN ALCOCK

Born in Worthing, a small seaside town in the south of England, Vivien Alcock's family moved to the country when she was ten. She later studied at the Ruskin School of Fine Arts at Oxford and then worked as a commercial artist in London for several years before she started writing full-time. She published her first novel for young adults—*The Haunting of Cassie Palmer*—in 1980, and *The Stonewalkers* the following year. She now lives in London with her husband, the writer Leon Garfield.

While only about a quarter of her writing is in the horror/supernatural genre, all of her work—most notably *The Cuckoo Sister* and *The Monster Garden*—has been written for young adults. She has published ten of her own short stories in *Ghostly Companions: A Feast of Chilling Tales*, in which the lives of normal people intersect with the "lives" of ghosts.

One of Vivien Alcock's recent books is *The Trial of Anna Cotman*, a story about a secret society at school and the power of ritual over the children who created it. To protect a young boy from being bullied, one girl breaks one of the society's rules and is put on trial for treason. Personal integrity is also the theme of *A Kind of Thief*, another of Alcock's recent novels. A family who has taken the father's honesty for granted is thrown into turmoil when he is arrested for embezzlement.

Although Ethan loved to spend time in his local library, getting lost in a book, he wasn't fond of the librarian. And with good reason. . . .

ETHAN UNBOUND

GARY L. BLACKWOOD

Ms. Morgan was a witch. At any rate she certainly looked like a witch. She wore baggy dresses and had stringy black hair and a pinched face, and if you could have stood to look into her beady eyes long enough, you would have seen that they were violet. With a little putty on her nose, she would have been a shoo-in for the Margaret Hamilton role in a revival of *The Wizard of Oz*.

Not only was she ugly, she was mean. Not in any big, shouting, physical way, but in little, underhanded, nasty ways. She was, in short, the sort of person who gives librarians a bad name.

Now, most librarians, as you know, are extremely pleasant and helpful people. Many are quite attractive and fashionable. Some even wear running shoes and know about such things as Nintendo and motor-driven skateboards.

Ms. Morgan was emphatically not one of this sort. If she knew anything about anything, she kept it to herself.

Ethan—the Ethan referred to in the title—was a bookworm. Not literally of course. If he had been an actual worm, Ms. Morgan would have long since searched him out and ground him beneath her heel. As it was, she only looked at him as if she'd like to.

Not that Ethan deserved it. He was a good kid, at least as teenagers go—a little on the klutzy side, a little too obsessed with grades, but on the whole pretty well liked. Except by Ms. Morgan. But then she didn't like anybody, probably not even herself.

You might expect that, being a librarian and all, Ms. Morgan would be partial to a boy like Ethan, who obviously loved books. He was even named after a book—a famous one written by Edith Wharton that had made his mother cry.

On the contrary, Ms. Morgan seemed to single him out for particular abuse. On those rare occasions when he brought a book back overdue, she charged him triple the usual fine. She sent him snide little reminders in the mail concerning books he'd checked out only two days before. When he couldn't avoid using the reference books, she kept her violet eyes pinned on him every second.

The sad fact of the matter was that Ms. Morgan, who had been attached to the library since long before Ethan was born, regarded each and every volume in the library as her private property and bitterly resented having to give them over into the hands of strangers.

With her piercing gaze, she examined each book that came back across the circulation desk, and heaven help anyone who was foolish or unlucky enough to return one with a smudged or, worse, a torn page. It was as though, in Ms. Morgan's eyes, the books were living things that could feel pain, and she fussed over a broken binding as a mother might over a child with a broken arm.

Ethan's fondness for books was a little less obsessive— though not much. He did have a few other interests— astronomy, for example, and bicycling—and he had three or four pretty good friends at school. But there was no denying that his best friends were the ones he met in books, and that very often the world he found in the pages of a book was more real and more comfortable for him than the actual world around him.

When he came across a really intriguing title on the shelves, sometimes he couldn't stand to wait until he got it home. He had to sit down with it right there in the aisle, on one of those little rolling stepstools, and an hour or two later, or three, when Ms. Morgan called out, in a whine not unlike that of a very large mosquito, "All right, everyone, the library is closing!" Ethan would come to, as if from a dream, and hurry to the circulation desk, where he pretended to tie his shoe, or examine the rack of large-print books, or anything to avoid the accusing stare of those violet eyes.

On the fateful night of which you are about to hear, Ethan was not in his usual spot in the Young Adult fiction. He had recently discovered an author named Heinlein, who was shelved in the adult books, and Ethan was so engrossed in something called *Tunnel in the Sky* that he shut out everything, including Ms. Morgan's insect whine. The thing that finally broke his concentration was every light in the entire library being switched off.

Startled, Ethan cried, "What?" and jumped to his feet. The only illumination in the big room was the red glow of the EXIT signs. The only sounds were the hum of the furnace blower somewhere in the bowels of the building and the feathery rustle of rain on the tall windows.

"Oh, man!" Ethan whispered to himself. "I'm locked in!"

Without even taking the time to reshelve the book in its proper place, he stumbled out of the stacks and down the center aisle to the main doors. As he had feared, they were locked tight.

"Crap!" he muttered, and gave the door a token kick with one sneaker.

The prospect of spending the night in the library wasn't so alarming. In fact for somebody who loved books as much as Ethan did, it was actually rather appealing. The thing that gave him pause was the thought that, when his dad got home, he wouldn't know where he was. Ethan was going to have to find a phone and call his dad at work.

He turned toward the librarian's desk—and found himself face-to-face with Ms. Morgan. "Aghh!" he said.

Ms. Morgan wore a shapeless raincoat and carried a black umbrella. In the light from the EXIT sign her eyes looked red. "Well, well," she said.

"I—I—" Ethan said.

"You got caught up in a book," Ms. Morgan said, not unkindly, "and you forgot the time, is that it?"

Ethan nodded—or was it a shudder?

"I'm not surprised. I knew it would happen sooner or later, a boy like you."

Ethan shifted about nervously. "Could I—could you—you know, let me out?" His voice cracked on the final word.

"In that downpour?" Ms. Morgan glanced sharply at the volume under his arm. "And with a *book*?"

Hastily Ethan clapped the book down on the desk. "I'll get it out another time," he said with a sickly smile.

"But surely," Ms. Morgan said, in a tone that would have sounded reasonable coming from someone else, "surely you don't want to get soaked to the skin. Couldn't your parents come for you?"

"Well, there's—there's just my dad, and he works late."

Ms. Morgan's eyes narrowed in what might have been construed as a smile. "What a shame. Perhaps you'd better stay, then."

"St-st-stay?"

Her raincoat rustled as she took a step toward him. "Of course. You like books, don't you?"

"Yes, but—"

"Well, then," she said, raising her umbrella as if she meant to impale him on the tip. "You should enjoy *being* one."

Ethan swallowed hard. "What?"

"I'll even give you your choice of what sort of book you'd like to be. What could be fairer?"

Ethan backed away, holding on to the edge of the desk for support. "I—I don't know what you mean." His hand groped for the telephone, but just as he lifted the receiver, Ms. Morgan's umbrella descended and, with a sharp whack, knocked it back onto the cradle.

"Come, come," she said, impatiently. "Where do you imagine that books come from? They don't grow on trees, you know."

Ethan clutched his stinging hand to his chest. "I—I thought you *bought* them someplace."

Ms. Morgan gave a derisive snort. "On the budget they give me?" She waved the umbrella. "Oh, I buy some things—series, joke books, that sort of nonsense. I'm talking about *good* books, books that last, books that seem *real*. They're not that easily come by, I promise you. They're not just written. They are *created*. The authors must put something of themselves into them." She took another step forward. "Sometimes *all* of themselves. Now, what will it be? Or shall I choose?"

"I—I really have to—"

"You remember Mr. Wise, the science teacher?"

Ethan blinked in bewilderment at this sudden change of topic. "The one that—that moved away a couple of years ago?"

Ms. Morgan wagged her umbrella at him. "No, no. He moved no farther away than my nonfiction section. He made quite an attractive book on physics."

Ethan put a hand to his muddled head. "This is crazy —I—"

"And you recall little Stephen Shelton, no doubt." She shook her head, making her plastic rain hat crinkle. "They searched for him high and low, when all they'd really have had to do was look in the picture books, under *S.*" She raised the umbrella again, and smacked it into the palm of her other hand. "But enough of that. Have you made up your mind yet? May I recommend a rousing adventure book? Or what about a historical novel? I don't really believe I'd care to have any more problem novels, they're so depressing—" She broke off abruptly, for Ethan, seeing that she was beyond a doubt either demented or dangerous, or both, had made a break for it.

"I thought you loved books!" he heard her screech behind him as he dived desperately into one of the narrow, darkened aisles between the shelves of the adult section. He scrambled to the far end, plunged across an open space, and rolled beneath one of the reading tables, where he crouched, his breath coming in quick, shallow bursts. He clamped his mouth shut and tried to breathe more quietly.

"Oho!" he heard Ms. Morgan cry. "That's the way it's going to be, is it? I must say, I'm disappointed in you. I thought you'd welcome the chance to *really* lose yourself in a book. But never mind. If you want to do it the hard way, that's all right too. You won't be the first. I'll just call up a little assistance.''

Assistance? Ethan thought. *Who would help a crazy woman?*

"Let me see," she was muttering. "Where are we? Mysteries, eh? Let's try under *D*. Ah, here we are. Doyle. Yes, this will do nicely." In her mosquito voice she called, "You see, my foolish friend, the spell works both ways. I can create books from life or"—a bright greenish spark, like a welding arc, lit up the part of the room where she stood—"life from books!" She laughed a manic laugh that was all but obscured by a sudden outburst of vicious barking and snarling. "Remember the Hound of the Baskervilles?" she shouted over the clamor. "Go get him, boy!"

Ethan heard the sound of claws scrabbling across the tile floor, and then, around the end of a set of shelves, a dark, four-legged form came thundering. It drew up short not five yards from the table where Ethan hid and stood quivering, swinging its huge head back and forth, sniffing the air.

Ethan didn't wait for the horrible hound to catch his scent; he shuffled backward on all fours, knocked over a chair with a heart-stopping crash, and, springing to his feet, took off at a run through the stacks. Behind him he heard the hound break into a frenzy of barking, and he knew he'd been spotted. He knew, too, that if he didn't do something drastic, the dog would be on him in a matter of seconds.

He darted behind the reference desk, fled past the magazine storage, and ran through an open door into the children's activity room. His impulse was to shut the door behind him, but he realized that if he did, he'd be trapping himself in the room. Instead he left the door ajar and burst through a second door that led to the children's collection, slamming that one shut behind him.

By the time he had circled through the children's department, past the magazines again, and back to the first door, the hound was inside the activity room, clawing at the door he'd just closed. Ethan banged the first door shut and leaned against it, his chest heaving, his legs like putty, while the hound, growling rabidly, flung itself against the inside of the door.

"Excellent!" Ms. Morgan's voice echoed through the big room. "I see you've learned how to use your library!"

Ethan guessed from her voice that she was still somewhere in the adult stacks. If he was right, that meant he had a clear shot at the front door. Taking a deep breath, he sprinted through the reference area, crashed into the freestanding globe, and recovered. A flash lit up the room behind him, but he made it to the main entrance without any interference.

He looked frantically around for something big enough to smash his way out with and settled on the electric typewriter that sat on Ms. Morgan's desk. She'd be furious—then again, what did it matter? Yanking the cord from the wall socket, he hefted the machine over his head. Before he could launch it through the window, something seized it from behind.

Ethan let go of the machine and whirled around to confront a figure who wore a black, batlike cape—but who he was pretty sure was not Batman. The caped figure tossed the typewriter carelessly aside and smiled a terrifying smile at Ethan—a smile that revealed two long, fanglike teeth.

"Oh, man!" Ethan groaned. "Dracula!"

"Ah, I see you've read my book," the figure said, in a thick accent. "Or," he added, distastefully, "more likely you've seen the movie. The book is much more worthwhile, I assure you. Perhaps you'd care to be a sequel?"

"No!" Ethan shouted, and bolted again. He wasn't really thinking very clearly, but he had a vague notion that he might be safer in the children's collection, where the books were not quite so threatening. He staggered past the picture books and into the nonfiction, where he flattened himself against the 700s and clung there, his mind and his heart racing.

Over the pounding of his own blood in his ears, he could hear footsteps approaching, passing the display case, moving through the picture books, pausing, heading into the fiction. In a minute or two more they would make their way back to the aisle where he was hiding.

There had to be some way out. He peered warily around the ends of the shelves. Obviously he couldn't escape through the activity room; he could still hear the Baskerville Hound thrashing and growling inside. He looked in the other direction and saw a pale red light high up on the wall. The emergency exit, of course. He had walked by it a hundred times, but, because of the sign that read in bold letters DO NOT OPEN EXCEPT IN EMERGENCY, it had never quite registered.

Well, if this wasn't an emergency, what was? Ethan slipped out from between the shelves and crept with painful slowness and care across the carpeted floor toward the EXIT sign.

He was less than six feet from it when a flash of green lit up the fiction stacks off to his right. Instinctively he threw up an arm to shield his eyes. When he lowered it, a new figure stood before him, blocking the exit, a bulky figure dressed in coarse, curious clothing from another century—a figure whose left leg ended above the knee, and who supported himself with a wooden crutch propped under one arm.

"So, lad!" the man said, in a booming voice. "About to jump ship, was you? By the powers, I can't make out why you'd want to do that and leave behind companions such as us!"

"Get out of my way!" Ethan shouted, his voice cracking with panic.

"Out of me way!" croaked the parrot that sat on the pirate's shoulder.

Ethan backed away and turned, ready to run again. But the dark, dread form of Dracula glided out from between the last two rows and stood in his way.

Frantic, he lunged down the aisle next to him, only to stop short as a third figure stepped into view at the far end of the aisle.

"Well, now," Ms. Morgan said, her raincoat rustling as she advanced on him. "That was fun, wasn't it? But it's time now to wind things up. Or should I say *bind* them up?" She gave a snorting laugh and extended her umbrella. "Don't worry," she said. "I'll do a very nice sewn binding, and of course you'll get only acid-free and recycled paper. You'll last for centuries. Why, you'll be practically immortal!"

As the tip of the black umbrella moved closer to his chest, in desperation Ethan yanked a book from the martial arts shelf next to him and flung it at the old woman's face. Shrieking, she jerked up the umbrella to ward it off.

The instant the book struck the umbrella, a fierce spark of green fire tore through the air, blinding Ethan. He staggered backward, out of the shelves and into the clutches of Long John Silver. "Too much grog, mate!" the parrot squawked.

Ethan squirmed out of the pirate's grasp and stumbled forward to find yet another figure confronting him—a lithe Asian man, barefooted and bare-chested, wearing only a loose pair of black pants. The man gave a perfunctory bow. "Bruce Lee," he said. "At your service."

Ethan beckoned frantically to him. "This way!"

Bruce Lee sprang out from between the shelves like a tiger and landed in a crouching karate stance before a very surprised Long John Silver.

"What's this, then?" boomed the pirate.

"Yahh!" said Bruce Lee.

"Look out!" said Ethan.

Before the words were fully formed, Bruce Lee had executed a 180-degree turn, and one of his bare feet was flashing through the air to intercept the dark form of Dracula, who had been about to launch an attack from the rear.

Dracula let out a rodentlike shriek and went flying backward. His slick-haired head bounded off a fire extinguisher, and he crumpled up like a Halloween bat made of black construction paper.

Bruce Lee whirled back around to face Long John— none too soon, for the pirate had raised his crutch aloft and sent it on a collision course with Lee's head.

But when it reached its target, the Asian man was no longer there; instead he was standing directly beside Silver, aiming a quick chop to the pirate's thick neck.

The startled parrot flapped away, squawking, "Out of me way," while Long John slumped heavily to the carpet.

Bruce Lee turned to Ethan with a small, satisfied smile. "Please," he said, "never tell anyone that I fought a man who had only one leg."

"I promise," Ethan said. He was about to add, "Let's get out of here," when he caught a glimpse of a dark, raincoated shape emerging from the shelves behind Lee. Before he could call out a warning, the old witch had raised her umbrella and launched it like a spear at Bruce Lee's bare back. As the tip of it struck him, a flash of green filled the room again.

Ethan fell back, rubbing at his eyes. When he opened them, Ms. Morgan was bending down to retrieve the umbrella with one gnarled hand and, with the other, a book featuring a colorful photo of Bruce Lee on the cover.

"I don't like it when books are out of their proper places," she said acidly. "And it's high time you were put in yours. You've been so much trouble to me, I believe I'll make a biography of you—one of those long, boring ones."

Ethan was almost past the point of caring. He was so tired of running, of resisting, that it sounded almost inviting to be put to rest between covers. But some part of him still protested, still insisted that it was better to live in the real world, with all its faults and stresses, than to sit stagnant on a shelf, cataloged and categorized.

"No!" he cried hoarsely and shrank back from the touch of the umbrella. He stumbled backward between the rows of books, clutching at volumes on either side, trying to keep from falling. But they gave way under his hands and tumbled from the shelves, and he kept staggering back and back until his heels struck against one of the rolling stepstools and he toppled over it and landed on his back in the aisle.

"I won't have my books treated this way!" screeched the old witch, and descended on him, her violet eyes wild.

With one foot Ethan sent the stool rolling at her, but she sidestepped it and came relentlessly on.

From the corner of his terrified eyes, Ethan caught a

glimpse of a shelf card that read OVERSIZED BOOKS. But no book could be big enough to protect him now. He needed something to defend himself with—a book about guns, or tanks, or—

Then his eyes fell on a familiar volume, one he'd read years before, a massive book with the title stamped in gold on the spine. Rolling on his side, he pulled it frantically from the shelf.

As Ms. Morgan's black raincoat loomed over him and, grinning gleefully, she extended her umbrella, Ethan yanked the book open to a vivid illustration and held it before him like a shield. The tip of the umbrella struck the page, and once again the blinding green spark exploded.

This time, when Ethan struggled to his feet, blinking and shaking his head, a figure stood before him that made Ms. Morgan's pinched face go tight and her violet eyes go wide in alarm. "You!" she breathed, her voice a long, low sigh of defeat.

"Aye, madam," said the white-robed figure, stroking his long gray beard with something like anticipation. "After all these centuries. And this time you've no beautiful enchantress to do your dirty work for you."

Ms. Morgan lowered her umbrella and took a few faltering steps back. "Now, Merlin," she said, in a tone Ethan had never heard from her before, a tone that was wheedling, pleading. "You had your day, I wanted mine, that's all."

"Fair enough, madam," said Merlin. "And now, it's over. Adieu."

Ms. Morgan opened her pinched mouth to protest, but the old wizard had raised his broad-sleeved arms, and a jagged white spark leaped across the gap between his fingers and her flinching form. The transformation was too sudden to be seen. One instant the old witch stood cowering in the aisle, the next there was nothing but a thick black volume lying on the carpet next to the other fallen books.

Merlin stooped to pick it up and handed it to Ethan. "There you are. A dubious addition to the library's collection."

Ethan stared at the old wizard, then at the cover of the book. It read, *The Memoirs of Morgan le Fay.*

"I wouldn't bother reading it if I were you," Merlin said. "You'll find it far too long and boring. You may as well go home now. I'll clean up here."

Ethan hesitated. "But—but there are things I want to ask you—"

Merlin waved a hand to dismiss him. "Ask your librarian," he said.

Ethan nodded vaguely, waved good-bye, and found his way to the main entrance. It was unlocked, and outside it had stopped raining.

When he got the nerve to visit the library again, a few days later, there was a new employee at the circulation desk—a kindly-looking old man with a neatly trimmed gray beard and a pair of running shoes.

GARY BLACKWOOD

Three of Gary Blackwood's four published novels have teen-agers as main characters. His first—*Wild Timothy*—was Recom-mended for Reluctant Readers by the American Library Associ-ation, and *The Dying Sun*—a futuristic novel about the onset of a new Ice Age—was named Best Young Adult Novel by Friends of American Writers in 1989.

Beyond the Door, his most recent novel, also employs a science fiction format. Like Ethan in "Ethan Unbound," the main character in *Beyond the Door* spends a lot of time in the library because he's certain that books will tell him the one single answer to what makes the universe work. By following a myste-rious man through a study room door, Scott finds himself in a parallel but more primitive world. Devoting himself to help bring about modernization on Gale'tin, Scott and his friend Tully find themselves in a life-and-death struggle when the world is threatened by new technology.

By shunning a lot of new technology, Gary Blackwood and his family have sought a simpler life on their eleven-acre home-stead in rural Missouri, where they have hand built an earth-sheltered twelve-sided house that is heated by wood cut by hand and powered by four photovoltaic panels. They are vege-tarians who garden organically and try to be as self-sufficient as possible.

When Holly and Jake promised to love each other forever, Jake really expected it to be forever. . . .

TLA

JANE MCFANN

I trudged down the hallway of Yannick High School, my nearly empty backpack bumping painfully against my still-sore spine. I should have felt light—happy, or at least relieved, but I didn't. I felt heavy, as if the effort required to lift one foot after another was more than should be asked of me. I thought I heard footsteps behind me, not quite footsteps but more like echoes of footsteps just slightly out of rhythm with my own. I turned to look down the long hallway, half expecting to see the math teacher whose classroom I had just left.

There was no one there.

Somehow I wasn't surprised. I walked out of the building, glad to escape the stale air. There's something almost eerie about a silent school long after the school day has ended, emptied of the shouting, thudding bodies. As usual my hand trembled as I searched through my book bag for the keys to the still-unfamiliar car my parents had insisted on buying for me.

"If you don't drive again now, you'll never be able to do it," they reasoned. I knew they were right, but that never stopped the trembling.

I tossed my book bag across the seat and slid behind the wheel. The bag was empty of its normal burden of textbooks. I'd turned them all in today, including the math one. Math had been the last test left to make up. All of my teachers had complimented me on my diligence in making up the two months' worth of work that I had missed. I should have been pleased. All that was left now was the graduation ceremony itself, five days from now.

I knew I should have been excited. Ever since I'd been a little girl, I'd dreamed about walking across the stage in cap and gown, wearing the yellow sash that designates an honors graduate.

At least my parents would be happy.

The book bag contained nothing but my filled-up notebooks and folders stuffed with old papers. Unused to its lightness, it slid off the seat and onto the floor of the passenger's side. I heard the thud of the one book it still contained, and I began to tremble harder.

I thought that I was going home to the bed I went to each day, a welcome destination for my back and my head and my leg that still ached fiercely. I refused to take the painkillers the doctor had given me. Somehow the pain seemed necessary.

I didn't go home. One turn after another after another, the car seemed guided in the opposite direction. I knew where I was going, even though I didn't want to go there.

I pulled the car onto the shoulder of the road, a remote turnoff that few had reason to discover. The road led to an area that once was a rock quarry but now was abandoned, leaving a sharp, tall cliff alongside the river. I could hear the rumbling of the small waterfall a few hundred yards downstream.

"There should be a guardrail here," I had said to Jake the first time he brought me here.

"Why?" he asked. "Anybody who chooses to come

here should be able to see the risk." He stepped closer to the edge. We were only fourteen then, and we had ridden our bicycles for miles to get there on a hot August afternoon. I could still see him as he was then—legs slender in worn jeans, T-shirt stuck to sweaty chest. The muscles would come a few years later when he discovered soccer and wrestling and that skinny body filled out.

I grabbed his arm and pulled him back from the edge.

"What?" he asked.

"You scare me that close to the edge," I said.

"Come here and look down," he said.

"No," I answered, trying to keep him back.

"Come here," he said. "It's beautiful. Trust me. I'll hold on to you. I won't let you fall."

I trusted Jake. I always had, ever since we met when we were ten years old. I let him take me to the edge. I didn't see the beauty that he saw when he looked down to the jagged rocks and rushing water, but I saw why it fascinated him. There was a power there, a ruthlessness that pulled him closer, and me with him. He locked his arms around me, and we stared into the water.

"Would you die if you fell?" I finally asked, my voice a whisper.

"Probably," he said. "If the rocks didn't get you, the waterfall would." There was no fear in his voice, but rather respect.

When he held me that day, I knew we'd never be childhood buddies again.

Everyone said they could never imagine us apart, probably because we so rarely were. HollyandJake—one word. My girlfriends envied me because I always had a boyfriend, always had a date to the movies or the prom or the game.

Except this year's prom of course.

HollyandJake. Every vision I ever had of my future included Jake. Even my parents had never told me to date others or complained that I was too young to get serious. In fact there were times when I accused them of loving him more than they loved me.

The only major argument Jake and I had, they sided with him. I got offered a scholarship at a school seven hundred miles away, and when I showed the letter to Jake, he screamed at me.

"How can you even consider taking that?"

"Jake, it's nice to be offered something like this."

"You mean you'd leave me? I can't believe you even applied there." Jake had no desire to go to college. His father owned a large farm, and all Jake had ever wanted to do was to work the land. He could make anything grow, calm any animal, accept any force of nature.

"I'll never leave you," I said. There was a certainty in me that I never would, a certainty mixed with just a touch of another feeling I couldn't quite identify.

Maybe sadness.

Maybe security.

I wrote the letter turning down the scholarship that same night. After all, the local university was good too.

"He's just a little insecure," my mother explained. "He's afraid that when you have a college degree and he doesn't, you'll outgrow him."

"I'll never outgrow him," I said, "but he can't stop me from growing in my own way."

"He knows that," my mother said. "He's just afraid."

"Jake's never afraid," I said. He was so sure of himself, so knowing about what he wanted.

A piece of land of his own.

Me.

Near the edge of the cliff there is a tree. Not just any

tree. My tree. It is a holly tree that soars at least forty feet into the air. Jake and I visited it in every season: in the spring when the new growth sprouts delicate and green, in summer when flocks of birds visit its prickly protection, in winter when red berries glow against the icy white of the snow.

"I can't believe it wasn't torn down by the quarrying," I said to Jake when we first noticed it.

"It was meant to be here for you," Jake said.

On my sixteenth birthday Jake took me there. He gave me a small box, carefully wrapped. I expected jewelry. What I got was a Swiss Army knife.

Jake must have seen the surprise on my face. "Wait. Let me explain," he said. He took me under the wide branches of the holly tree and pointed to a smooth place on the trunk. "There. Right there," he said.

I understood. I opened the largest blade on the knife, and carefully, painstakingly carved a heart into the trunk of the holly tree. Inside the heart I carved:

> Holly
> and
> Jake
> TLA

True Love Always.

In the next years that's what Jake would murmur to me at the end of a long, sleepy, late-night telephone conversation. That's what he would whisper after our last kiss.

I ducked under the branches of the holly tree, hauling my book bag with me, and traced the heart and the letters over and over again with my fingers.

TLA.

I sat on the ground, sweeping away the prickly leaves,

and finally, trembling so badly that I could barely work
the zipper, I opened my book bag and took out the one
remaining book.

I'd only gotten the book that morning. I ran my fingers
over the red, rough-textured cover with the smooth gold
embossed seal of the school. I didn't want to open it, but
I had to. It was a new pain to be faced, a pain that I had
to endure, deserved to endure.

TLA.

I opened the cover of the yearbook and paged through
it methodically. Page after page brought images of Jake.

Soccer team.

In a crowd shot of a pep fest.

Leaning against a doorway, smiling that slightly
crooked smile of his.

He and I in the Senior Superlatives section: Senior-
Class Couple.

Jake by himself: Best Looking.

Me by myself: Most Likely to Succeed.

HollyandJake, holding hands in the hallway.

People didn't envy me much these days. In fact they
didn't even talk to me much. I knew it was because they
didn't know what to say. I knew it was because they were
afraid of saying the wrong thing. I knew it was because I
wasn't exactly a sparkling conversationalist myself these
days.

"She's still in a lot of pain," I heard them whisper in
the hallway.

"It just doesn't seem right to see Holly without . . ."

And then there was the other whisper I heard at night
when I stared into the darkness.

TLA.

And the footsteps that I heard behind me in quiet hall-
ways when there was nobody there.

TLA.

"Jake would want you to go on with your life," my mother said. "He would want you to be happy."

"Don't ever leave me," I heard him whisper, with a refrain that sounded like wind blowing through a holly tree or distant water flowing over rocks.

My fingers traced his senior picture in the yearbook. I never liked it that much. He looked uncomfortable in a coat and tie, and there was no sign of that slightly crooked smile that had helped me grow up. When I thought of Jake, I saw him in old jeans worn thin and nearly white at the knees and a red plaid flannel shirt, his hands dirty, his face aglow.

"Look, Holly. The first flowers are open on the honeysuckle. Isn't that the sweetest smell in the world? Come here, Holly. Smell the honeysuckle."

And I would smell the honeysuckle, and I would smell the healthy, earthy, sweaty smell of Jake, and I could not tell which was sweeter.

I shivered despite the warmth of early June, and I shut the yearbook. The pain in my back intensified, but I refused to shift my position.

"Why won't you take the pain medicine?" my mother recently asked, the pain in her eyes mirroring the pain in mine. "You don't have to punish yourself. You know it wasn't your fault. You *do* know that, don't you?"

That's what the police told me. The car that hit us was driven by an old man who had had a heart attack and veered wildly into our lane, not giving me a moment to react. I'd had my seat belt on, and I'd awakened in the hospital with no memory of the accident except the back and head and leg injuries.

"Jake?" I said as soon as I regained consciousness. "Jake?"

"Take it easy," my mother said, and a nurse immediately stuck a needle in my arm. I was sure, as I slipped into darkness, that Jake was beside me, holding my hand.

"Jake," I murmured drowsily the next time I awoke.

"Holly, there's something you need to know," my mother said.

"No," I said, knowing what she was going to say. "He's here with me."

That was the first time I heard the whisper.

TLA.

I sat under the holly tree and picked up some of the leaves, closing my fingers over them, deliberately letting the sharp points puncture my skin.

If I hadn't wanted to go to that party . . .

If I hadn't insisted on driving . . . Jake was a better driver than me. Maybe he could have swerved.

If I had made him put on his seat belt. That was the big one. I'd fussed at him before about that, but he always said a seat belt kept him too far away from me.

"Never leave me. Promise you'll never leave me."

Doctors claim that the will to live is important. I got better anyway. My body, young and strong, healed, leaving only the pain behind.

"You're lucky not to have any scars," one girl said. After she saw the look on my face, she, too, stopped talking to me.

I slowly rose off the ground beneath the holly tree. I thought I was going to the car, but I wasn't. I walked to the edge of the drop-off and looked down. The water rushed busily over the jagged rocks; the waterfall made the water thrash a few hundred yards downstream.

TLA, came the whisper. It could have been the wind or the water, but it wasn't.

I looked over the edge, curiously unafraid. I put down

my book bag, its notebooks and folders a part of life as far away as childhood.

TLA.

I held the yearbook in both hands, feeling its weight, watching the filtered afternoon sun glint off the gold of the school emblem.

TLA, came the whisper. *Don't ever leave me.*

I held out the yearbook and opened my hands, watching it fall. It fell swiftly and gracefully, no fluttering pages, no hesitation. It hit once on the jagged gray rocks and then was swept away by the water.

Don't ever leave me, came the whisper.

I knew what I was supposed to do. I knew it as deeply and as certainly as I knew that Jake loved me.

"No," I said. "Let me grow in my own way."

TLA, came the whisper.

TLA.

What future could ever be complete or happy without Jake? How could I spend the rest of my life with half a heart, half a soul, and no slightly crooked smile to guide me?

Trust me, said the whisper.

I always had.

"Are you sure?" I said, my voice quiet but calm.

TLA, came the answer.

I leaned over the water, trying to give myself to the whisper. I leaned until my muscles screamed in agony. I willed myself to let go.

In the last second before I let go, I smelled something very familiar. It was honeysuckle, and mixed with it was a strong, earthy, sweaty smell.

"No, Jake," I said, pulling back a step. "I have to stay for a while longer. I have to smell the honeysuckle. I have to grow a little more. For you. And for me."

Never leave me, said the whisper, fading softer and softer, lost in the slightest touch of the breeze.

"I won't," I said. "As long as there is honeysuckle, I'll never leave you."

JANE MCFANN

"TLA" is Jane McFann's first foray into stories with a supernatural connection. Her novels for young adults are usually rooted in reality, with scenes occurring in school settings, probably because that's what she knows best, since she is an English teacher at Glasgow High School in Newark, Delaware. "For me, teaching young adults as well as writing for them is a wonderful combination," she says.

The first two of Jane McFann's eight novels for young adults are among her best-known works. *Maybe by Then I'll Understand* is the story of the troubled relationship between a sixteen-year-old girl and a boy she can't resist; its sequel, *One More Chance,* adds Bulldozer Boy, a strange newcomer whom only Cath tries to understand.

In McFann's most recent novels a high school girl decides to pursue the truth about a friend's death, even when that places Cath in conflict with her best friend and her first love in *One Step Short.* And in *No Time for Rabbits* five kids, an ancient history teacher who may be dying, and a loose rabbit are trapped in a high school by an ice storm—with both funny and dramatic results.

In addition to owning pet rabbits herself, Jane McFann is interested in digging in the dirt, listening to music, and "always searching for new ways to learn, grow, and create."

ELECTRIFIED

It's bad enough that Will has always been afraid of electrical storms. Now he's about to be left in the dark with a frightful companion. . . .

FOR PETE'S SNAKE

ELLEN CONFORD

The last, tearful words my sister, Petra, said to me as they drove her off to the hospital were, "Please, Will, take care of my Coily!"

It was Saturday evening, on the Fourth of July weekend. My parents didn't know how long they'd have to wait in the emergency room. But they were used to it. This was not the first time Pete had fallen out of a tree. Or off the roof. Or off her skateboard.

Pete is a major klutz. She breaks things. Mostly her bones. Whenever anyone asks my father for a credit card, he says, "Visa, American Express, or County General?"

So there was really nothing new about Pete being carried off to the hospital again.

Except that this time I had promised to baby-sit a boa constrictor.

Well, I hadn't really promised. But I had nodded. I'm her brother, what else could I do? The kid was in pain, in tears, and in the car. If I'd said no, she might have jumped out of the car and tried to take Coily with her to the hospital. Then my mother and father would probably have argued over who would get to shoot me.

And besides, I thought, as I sat down on the front

steps, it's a snake, not a baby. It's not as if I'd have to pick him up, or rock him, or burp him or anything.

As Pete told my mother when she begged to adopt the beast, "They're really no trouble at all. You don't have to walk them, and you only have to feed them every two weeks. And they eat mice."

"We don't have any mice," my mother had pointed out.

"So we'll get some," Pete said.

The sky was beginning to turn a coppery color, and I could see hard-edged dark clouds on the horizon. The air was heavy and still. I hoped we weren't going to have a thunderstorm.

It's not that I'm really afraid of storms. It's just that when I was five, I wandered away from our tent during a family camping trip. I got lost, and this monster thunderstorm came up—

Well, ever since then I've been a little tense about thunder and lightning.

Except for the occasional sound of a distant firecracker, the neighborhood was unnaturally quiet. A lot of people were away for the holiday weekend, and the others were at Waterside Park, waiting for the fireworks display.

Which is where we were planning to go before Petra fell out of the tree.

I can go anyway, I realized. After all, it wasn't as if I had to do anything for Coily. Mostly he lay on the flat rock in his tank, or wrapped himself around the tree branch in there, or hid inside the copper water pipe Pete had found for him.

"They like to hide," Pete explained. "Where they can't be seen."

"Great," I'd told her. "The less I see him, the better."

Not that I'm afraid of snakes—but, hey, even Indiana Jones thinks they're repulsive. So I'd just look in on Coily —very briefly—and then go off to see the fireworks. If I could find someone to drive me.

I went into the house, flipping on light switches as I made my way to the kitchen. It was getting pretty dark. The fireworks would probably begin in about an hour.

I phoned my friend Josh, hoping he was home.

"Hey, Will!" he shouted. "Boy, am I glad to hear somebody who doesn't sound like Popeye the Sailor Man."

"Excuse me?"

"There's a six-hour Popeye marathon on cable. We're into the fourth hour here."

"Then you'll be glad to know why I'm calling," I said. "Though it does involve water." I explained about Pete and the hospital, and about how I wanted to go down to Waterside Park.

"That would be great," he said.

"Okay, come over and pick me up and—"

"Except that I have to sit with Steffie." Steffie is Josh's five-year-old sister.

"Bring her along," I said.

"She's got a strep throat," Josh said. "I can't take her anywhere."

"It's hot out," I said. "It wouldn't hurt her to just lie on a blanket and watch—"

"She's got a hundred-and-one fever," he said. "Hey, I have to go. I think I hear her croaking for something. Enjoy the fireworks."

"How can I—" But he'd already hung up. How can I enjoy the fireworks, I'd been about to ask, with no one to drive me there? The park is four miles away.

Shelly! I thought. My friend Shelly had a brand-new

driver's license and was always looking for an excuse to drive somewhere.

I heard a lot of noise in the background when Mrs. Getz answered the phone. Kid noise. Like a bunch of preteenies squealing and giggling.

"Hi, Mrs. Getz. It's Will. May I speak to Shelly?"

"She's sort of tied up at the moment," said Mrs. Getz. "Can she call you back?"

"What's going on there?" I asked. "Is that Shelly screaming?"

"I think so," Mrs. Getz answered. "She's supposed to be running Carol's birthday party." Carol is Shelly's eleven-year-old sister.

"I forgot about the party," I said glumly. "I guess she'll be tied up for a while then."

"She will until I go untie her," said Mrs. Getz. "I believe they're playing Joan of Arc."

"Boy," I said, thinking of Pete and Steffie, "kids can sure be a pain sometimes."

Mrs. Getz snorted. "Tell me about it," she said, and hung up.

I dropped the phone back on the hook. I peered out the window over the kitchen sink. It was only seven thirty, but the darkness was closing in fast.

I called three other friends. Two weren't home. Chip, the third, had to shout over the sound of an electric guitar, and some horrible wailing.

"Family reunion!" he yelled. "That's my cousin Dennis."

"What's he doing?"

"Elvis Presley. Why don't you come over? We're barbecuing."

"Dennis, I hope," I muttered.

"What? I can't hear you."

"I said, great, I'll be right there." It was only half a mile to Chip's, and even if I'd have to listen to Dennis, it was better than sitting alone in the house with a boa constrictor.

And then I heard a distant rumble.

"Was that thunder?" I asked.

"I can't hear a thing," Chip shouted. "Dennis is doing 'Hound Dog.' "

Another rumble. Closer.

"I think it's starting to rain," Chip said. "It doesn't matter. Come on over."

"Well, maybe not," I said. "I mean, if it's raining."

"That's okay. We'll go inside. Whoo, there goes the lightning."

"I'd better stay here," I said. "My folks might try to call."

"Oh, yeah," Chip said. "You have this thing about thunderstorms."

"I do *not* have a thing about thunderstorms," I said defensively. "I just don't feel like walking half a mile in a downpour, that's all." With lightning striking all around me.

"Suit yourself," Chip said. "I'd better help Dennis get his amp inside before he's electrocuted."

"Right." I slammed the phone down. Okay. Fine. I'll stay home. I'll read. I'll watch TV. I'll listen to music. I'll worry about my sister.

I'll be alone in the house with a boa constrictor.

Big deal. It doesn't scare me. All he ever does is lie on his rock. Or curl up inside his pipe. I won't bother him, he won't bother me. I'm not really afraid of snakes anyway. I just happen to find them repulsive, disgusting, and evil looking.

But I'm not afraid of them.

And I'm certainly not afraid of being alone in the house. And even though it's starting to thunder, I'm perfectly safe, as long as I don't talk on the telephone, stick my toe in a light socket, or stand under a tree.

So there's nothing to be afraid of. Even if it is getting so dark that the light over the kitchen table is barely making a dent in the gloom.

So don't stay in the kitchen, dummy, I told myself. There's a whole, brightly lit house to wander around in. I'll just go check the stupid snake, I thought, then settle down in front of the TV. There's nothing like a Popeye festival to calm your nerves.

I turned on the light in the hallway and headed toward Pete's room.

One quick look into the glass tank and I could say that I'd kept my promise. Coily will be curled up on his rock, and I'll go curl up with Popeye and Olive. The rumbles of thunder that had seemed so far away a moment ago were louder now. The storm was coming closer.

That's okay, I told myself. The closest thing to a tree in this house was Coily's branch, and I would hardly climb into the tank and wedge myself under it, so there was nothing to worry about.

The door to Pete's room was wide open. This was a major violation of rules. Ever since she'd gotten the boa, Pete had strict orders to keep her door closed. That way, in case Coily ever managed to escape from his tank, he'd be confined to Petra's room and be reasonably easy to recapture.

Not that any of us, except Pete, would ever try to recapture him. My father said, "If that thing gets loose, I'm moving to a motel and putting the house up for sale."

So far the only time the snake had been out of Pete's room was when she would occasionally drape Coily around her shoulders and parade around the house so we could admire his exotic markings and alleged tameness.

When Pete "walked" her scaly pet, the rest of us found urgent business to attend to in rooms with doors that locked.

Anyway, it disturbed me that Pete's door was wide open, but I figured that in her hurry to get to the yard and climb a tree so she could fall out of it, she'd forgotten the rule.

I reached inside the room and flicked the light on. From the entrance I peered at the snake tank. It was a large, glass rectangle with gravel on the bottom and plastic mesh screening over the top. Pete had taped a little sign on the side that said COILY'S CORNER.

I couldn't see the beast at first, but that didn't throw me. As Pete had said, snakes like to hide, so I figured Coily was scrunched inside his copper pipe.

I moved into the room. A clap of thunder made me jump, but it wasn't too bad, and I didn't see any lightning flash.

"Miles away," I reassured myself. "Just get the stupid snake check over with and go watch something dumb on the tube."

Okay. I cleared my throat so Coily would know I was coming and not feel he had to rear up and do anything dramatic to protect his territory. I know snakes can't hear. But why take chances?

I edged closer to the tank. I could see it all, the whole thing. But I couldn't see Coily. Inside the pipe, I reminded myself. Just squat down, look inside the pipe, barf, run out of the room, and shut the door.

The lights flickered with another burst of thunder.

Lights flicker in a storm, I reminded myself. No need to panic. I squatted down and looked into the copper pipe.

I could see clear through it to the other side. There was nothing inside it but air.

"Yikes!" I straightened up, and as I did, I noticed that the plastic mesh screening on top of the tank had a jagged rip in one corner.

As if something—something with fangs—had gnawed right through it.

"Yikes!" I was repeating myself, but this was no time to worry about being clever. I raced out of Pete's room and slammed the door. I leaned against the wall, panting, even though I'd only sprinted ten feet.

What a narrow escape. I could have been standing—or squatting—right there in front of the tank, with the boa lurking under a chair just waiting to slink up and constrict me.

And then it hit me.

Pete's door had been open when I went into her room. It had been open for almost an hour. The snake might not be in there at all. In fact it could be anywhere in the house by this time.

I hugged the wall, wanting to climb up it. If I could hang from the light fixture on the ceiling, chances were the creature couldn't reach me.

Don't lose it, Will, I told myself. This is stupid. I could see all the way up and down the hall, and the boa was nowhere in sight.

There are seven rooms in this house, I reminded myself. Plus the hall. The odds are eight to one that I won't be in the same place as the snake. As long as I keep my eyes open—

Two deafening bursts of thunder, one right on top of the other. Instinctively I shut my eyes and clapped my hands over my ears. Then I thought of the twelve-foot-long snake slithering along the hall toward me. I snapped my eyes open and did a 360 to make sure I was still alone.

Another clap of thunder. The lights went out.

"No!" I yelled. *"No!* Don't let the electricity go off!"

The lights came back on.

"Thank you."

A drenching rain began to pound the house. It sounded as if I were standing in the middle of Niagara Falls.

Flashlight! I thought. Candles. Quick, while I could still find them.

I ran for the kitchen. I opened the utility cabinet, next to the refrigerator. Something smacked against the window. It was probably a branch of the mimosa tree, driven by a sudden, howling wind that had seemed to come from nowhere.

"Just the tree," I told myself. "It happens all the time when it's windy."

As I turned around to make sure it was nothing more sinister than the tree branch, the room went black.

Another flicker. I tried to keep calm. The electricity would come back on in a moment.

But it didn't.

"Aw, no!" I begged. "Not the lights. A boa constrictor and a thunderstorm aren't enough for one night?"

As if in ironic answer, a flash of lightning—very close, *extremely* close—illuminated the room with a harsh, chalky light. For three seconds I could see as clearly as if it were daytime. The mimosa tree, the sink, the white curtains at the window . . .

And the giant brown reptile twined around the curtain rod flicking his forked tongue at me.

I screamed and jumped backward, crashing against the

open door of the utility cabinet. Shrieking, I stumbled out of the kitchen, flailing my arms in front of me to keep from banging into anything else.

Which didn't work. I tripped over the stepladder, bounced off a wall, and staggered into the dining room, where I met the china cabinet head-on. Every dish on the shelves clattered as I careened into it and landed on the floor. I moaned, and wondered which part of my body hurt the most.

I sat huddled there for a moment, dazed and whimpering. Now, accompanying the torrential rain, there was a loud, rattling sound, as if someone were hurling handfuls of gravel against the windows. Hail, I thought. You sometimes get hail with severe thunderstorms. And tornadoes.

Great. A tornado. Just what I need. Thunder and lightning and hail and total darkness and a wandering boa constrictor and a tornado.

Mommy!

The hail and rain were making so much noise that I could hardly hear myself think. If you could call what I was doing thinking. If I can't hear myself think, I realized, I can't hear the brown monstrosity unwind himself from the curtain rod.

I can't hear him slip down off the sink, and across the floor, and out of the kitchen, and into the dining room, where I'm curled up here on the floor like a sitting—

"Ayiee!"

I leaped to my feet—or at least I crawled to my knees and stood up as quickly as I could with an entirely black-and-blue body. *Think, Will,* I ordered myself. *Just shut the kitchen door, and—*

Good idea. Except we don't have a kitchen door, only an archway that separates the kitchen from the dining room. At this very moment Coily could be slithering past the refrigerator, heading for the dining room.

I'll go to my room. I'll go to my room and shut the door. No problem. Just grope around the table, through the living room, down the hall, and into my room. I can certainly move faster than a snake can slither—at least I can when the lights are on.

Of course there is another archway that leads from the kitchen and into the hall. The snake could be creeping out that way and into the hall just as I—

Don't even think about it.

Move.

I moved. As fast as I could, in the dark, with only an occasional flash of lightning to help me around the maze of furniture that clutters the living room.

"Why is this room so crammed?" I wondered, as I banged my shin against a footstool. "Does anyone really need this much furniture?"

I flung my arm against a plant stand. A flowerpot crashed to my feet.

"Please don't let it be my mother's African violet that didn't bloom for three years up until last week," I prayed.

I made it to my room without further damage to myself or to our overfurnished house. I slammed the door behind me. I was sure the snake couldn't have gotten to my room before I did.

Well, I was pretty sure.

Call Josh, I thought. *Maybe his parents are home by now. Maybe he can come over with a flashlight, find the boa, and put him back in his tank.*

The phone next to my bed has a lighted keypad, which is convenient if you have to call the police in the middle of the night, or if a boa constrictor gets loose in the dark.

When Josh picked up his phone, I didn't even say hello. I just shrieked.

"You have to come over and help me! I don't know where Coily is!"

"Did you check with Larry and Moe?" he asked.

"*What?*"

"A Three Stooges joke," he explained. "You know, Larry, Moe, and—"

"This is no time for jokes!" I yelled. "I'm alone in the house with a rampaging boa constrictor, and the lights are off, and—"

"I can't take my sister out in this storm," he cut in.

"When will your parents be home?" I asked desperately.

"Monday," he answered.

"ARRGGHH!" I slammed down the phone.

There was only one thing to do. Only one intelligent, mature way of coping with the situation.

I dived into bed and pulled the covers over my head.

The snake couldn't be in my room. He just couldn't be. I'd be perfectly safe here under the covers. If I didn't pass out from the heat or smother myself.

I cowered there, sweating and shaking, waiting for my parents to come home. Once in a while I'd think I'd heard a car door slam. Then I'd poke my head out and listen. And gasp for air. But the only sounds were the rain —softer now—and distant rumbles of thunder.

I don't know how long I stayed there, trying to breathe, feeling my clothes getting wetter and wetter with sweat, telling myself that there was no snake in my room and that even if there was, he preferred curtain rods to beds.

And then I felt something soft graze my leg.

For a moment I froze. I couldn't breathe, couldn't even scream, which is what I really wanted to do.

It can't be a twelve-foot boa constrictor, I told myself. *It's just a beetle or a mosquito or something.* But it didn't feel like a beetle or a mosquito.

It felt like a wet strand of spaghetti crawling up my leg.

I threw the covers off, howling. Just as I did, the electricity came back on. My room blazed with light. I blinked, and like a kid waking up from a nightmare, clutched my pillow to my chest. I forced myself to look down, down toward the end of the bed, where I had flung off the covers.

And saw a procession of brown, foot-long snakes writhing up my sheet, heads darting, tongues flicking, coming straight at me.

Screaming uncontrollably, I threw myself out of bed. I could still feel something on my leg. When I looked down, I saw that one of the creatures was hanging from my ankle like a loose boot strap.

"NO! *NO!*" I shook my leg violently, and the snake fell to the floor. I felt as if there were snakes crawling all over my body. I twisted around frantically, smacking my pillow against my legs, my arms, my chest.

What if they're in my shorts?

I screamed even louder, dropped my pillow, and scrambled out of my cutoffs. Through my screaming I heard feet pounding down the hall.

"Will! *Will!*" My father threw my door open and grabbed me by the shoulders.

"Snakes! Snakes!" I screamed. "In my pants! In my bed!"

My mother was right behind him. Dimly, through a haze of terror, I saw Pete peer into my room. She had a splint on one arm and a boa constrictor wrapped around the other.

"How come you're running around in your under—" She looked over at my bed.

"Coily!" she cried delightedly. "You're a girl!"

Maybe the biggest surprise was that my hair did *not* turn completely white. Although I was afraid to look in a mirror for two days.

Coily has been adopted by one of my sister's weird friends. My mother put her foot down. She told Pete, "Look, your brother cannot live in the same house with that snake."

"So let him move," Pete said.

They think they found all the babies. But since no one knows how many snakes Coily actually gave birth to, no one is positive they're really all gone. Pete says if there are any left, they ought to come out pretty soon, because they'll be hungry.

In the meantime they could be anywhere. In the pipes under the toilet, in the back of a closet, behind the refrigerator.

So I did move. I'm staying at Josh's house for a while. My parents have been very understanding about my traumatic experience. Especially my father.

He's checked into a motel for two weeks.

ELLEN CONFORD

Since publishing *Impossible, Possum* in 1971, Ellen Conford has written more than thirty books for children and young adults, all of which contain a great deal of humor. "I want to make them laugh," she says. In addition to laughs, her books have earned her a number of awards, among them the IRA/ CBC Children's Choice Award, the 1983 California Young Reader Medal, and a Parent's Choice Award for Literature.

Among her popular novels for teenagers are *Dear Lovey Hart, I Am Desperate; Seven Days to a Brand New Me; A Royal Pain;* and *Hail, Hail Camp Timberwood,* a novel based entirely on her own experiences. She also has published one collection of her own short stories, called *If This Is Love, I'll Take Spaghetti,* and is currently working on a second collection, tentatively titled *I Love You, I Hate You, Get Lost.* Although she loves to read mysteries, she hasn't yet attempted to write one—but stay tuned. . . .

Her most recent novel is *Loving Someone Else,* about a formerly wealthy seventeen-year-old girl who has to take a job as companion-maid-chauffeur to two old ladies in order to raise money for college.

Ellen Conford lives with her professor husband in Great Neck on Long Island, New York, where she spends her spare time reading, watching old movies, collecting cookbooks, and competing in Scrabble and crossword-puzzle tournaments.

Aunt Florrie ruined every Christmas for forty years. Will this one finally be different . . . ?

AUNT FLORRIE

ROBERT WESTALL

I've been helping my dad write Christmas cards. He has such lovely ones. Blond female Santas in miniskirts. Ones with reindeer so drunk they can't pull the sleigh. My father is an Importer of Novelties. Our house is lovely, too, at the moment. Ten-foot tree; holly and ivy and mistletoe everywhere, and they're all plastic. My mum is ever so happy there are no needles and bits to Hoover up.

Anyway, there sits my dad, crossing people off his Christmas-card list because they didn't send him one last year, or they've gone bankrupt or something. But he *has* got a heart.

"I'm wondering whether to send one to Old Charlie Harris," he says out loud. "I've not seen him since we left school in 1970, but he never forgets to send me one, especially since I got a bit famous. Can't be much fun for Charlie, enduring life in Liverpool Eight, with six kids and no job. Don't know how he can afford to send cards, on the dole. But I'll not consign him to oblivion. Not for the price of a twenty-pence card and a nineteen-pence stamp. It's probably all he gets for Christmas." And he pulls the smallest of his cards toward him, the one with the smudge on the back, and sits with his pen poised, wondering what to say that will cheer up Charlie.

"At least you won't have to send one to Aunt Florrie," I said to him. "Now that she's dead and safely buried." I said it with great Christmas thankfulness. You see, our family is not exactly a close one; we don't get together much, even at Christmas. There are Difficulties. I mean, my uncle Sammy is loaded, but he's a bookmaker, and not quite nice, and his wife is Catholic and pious and talks about Baby Jesus in the most embarrassing way, just when everybody's getting sloshed and having a really good time. And Uncle Henry is a Methodist and doesn't hold with drinking at all. And Uncle Tommy has got an embarrassing car with rust around the bottom that would look just awful parked outside the house; one of the neighbors might complain about it to the Council and have it towed away. And Aunt Cissie lives in Bootle, and the rest are just . . . well . . . poor. So we never saw anyone over Christmas.

Except Aunt Florrie, who'd invited herself to our house for Christmas Day every year for forty years. It started with my dead-soft departed grandparents, who never had the guts to tell her she wasn't wanted.

Aunt Florrie always arrived early, and her mouth was going full out even before you opened the front door to her. Probably telling the plants in the front garden to stand up straight and stop slouching because the weather wasn't all *that* cold. She would look at my father with her cold green fishy eyes, give him a whiff of her breath, which always smelt of fish too, and tell him his front path needed weeding. Then she would step inside and just stand, laden with her handbag and her umbrella and what she called her bits and pieces, until everybody ran to take things off her and help her off with her hat and coat. And she would tell whoever went to hang up her coat to fetch a hanger, otherwise they would give the coat a nasty, unsightly bump on the shoulders.

Then she would spread herself on the three-seater finest English-leather Chesterfield in the lounge so that nobody else would be able to sit there for the whole of Christmas Day, and me and Stan, my brother, would have to sit on hard chairs brought from the dining room. Honestly, I don't know how she managed to fill that settee, even allowing for her massive pear-shaped body with her huge gray-clad thighs under a skirt that was constantly riding up to show off more than it should. From which all our family averted their eyes like it was the End of the World or some other Cosmic Disaster.

I used to wonder desperately if any male, even in the deepest depths of past time, had ever enjoyed looking up Aunt Florrie's skirt. But she has her son, Albert, to prove it, so somebody must once have done it.

Anyway, she would fill the rest of the settee with her handbag and her bits and pieces; the amorphous bundle of gray knitting that she never worked on and that never seemed actually to grow into anything from one Christmas to the next; and a huge crumpled paper bag of mints, which she chewed continuously when we weren't giving her something else to chew, and which frequently spilled its contents all over the floor, rolling into the far corners of the room, and which she expected us all to rush to pick up at least twice an hour. Then there were her holiday photographs from Benidorm the previous summer (or was it the summer before that? They always seemed the same to me; she always went to Benidorm and photographed the same fat friends in front of the same pointless objects). These she insisted on passing around like holy relics during the exciting bits of *The Poseidon Adventure and* wasn't satisfied till we'd made some comment like "That's a lovely drainpipe," which I swear I once heard my father say.

She talked nonstop, even during the Queen's Speech, when she said things like "I think she's put on weight this year" or "She sits behind the desk to hide her varicose veins, poor thing."

Her voice could drown the telly even when it was turned up full, the way Maria Callas could drown the chorus at La Scala in Milan. And there was no escaping into other rooms to watch the telly, even for Stan and me. (We have tellies in every room and a videotape machine in most, except the bathrooms, where my father says it would be dangerous.) No, she would come rooting us out if we were gone for more than three minutes, saying Christmas was the time when the whole family should be together. Once our Stan even dragged a portable into the downstairs loo, and she was hammering on the door of that, and he was shouting back that he had bad constipation, and she began threatening him with senna pods. . . .

At the dinner table she always had three helpings of everything, helping herself with a little smile and simper so as not to bother anybody, even before anybody else had been offered seconds. The only time she stopped chewing was to adjust her false teeth with three loud clicks, or to say things to my mother like "I see you've bought a smaller turkey this year" or "Is this a Sainsbury's pudding? I've never liked Sainsbury's puddings."

By midnight on Christmas Day, when she would finally go, my father would be sloshed to the gills and my mother spacing out intermittently. So that when Aunt Florrie said, with her fiendish grin, "See you again next year!" they were only able to grin back and nod weakly.

And thank the Lord for the other three hundred and sixty four Florrie-less days of the year. . . .

So you can imagine our feelings when, a week before Christmas two years ago, Aunt Florrie was terminated by a double-decker bus while coming out of Lime Street Station without looking. My father said he never went to a funeral more gladly in his whole life. He even paid twice what he meant to for a wreath, out of sheer relief that she was at last underground and a real Christmas could begin, the first in forty years.

Mind you, it was a quiet Christmas, that one. Just the family: Mam, Dad, Stan, and me. Dad had left it too late to invite anyone else around to share our post-Florrie paradise. But it was like the Kingdom of Heaven, even if our Stan was sick through gobbling too many liqueur choccies.

The next year (last year, that is) my dad was on the verge of inviting all and sundry, when a Christmas card arrived. A small, mean envelope of thin, gray, hairy paper that stood out among all the posh ones he got from his business associates, each trying to outdo the others with huge all-shiny-red cards with gold holly, or all-gold cards that played "Jingle Bells" when you opened them, or comic ones of Santa going down the crematorium chimney by mistake.

As I said, a small, mean envelope. The kind Aunt Florrie used to send, I was thinking, when we looked down and saw the handwriting.

It was Aunt Florrie's writing. There was no mistaking that small, vicious, spidery script. The best forger in the world would rather try a Bank of England fiver than Aunt Florrie's handwriting. Inimitable.

With trembling fingers, my father opened it. It was indeed signed "Love from Aunt Florrie" and even had three horrid little *x*'s. And in the corner it said "See you as usual on Christmas Day."

The postmark was two days before.

"There must be some mistake," said my mother in a voice that suggested that the greenhouse effect was knocking on our front door at the very moment.

Dad ran out of the front door with the card and envelope into his Jag and was gone for three hours.

When he came back, he said, "It's no forgery. The police got their handwriting expert on to it. He compared it with those letters of complaint she was always writing to them, about dog dirt in Lime Street. They'd never got around to clearing them out of their files. And the bloke said the ink was pretty new too."

You may wonder why the police were so helpful. All I can say is that, as an Importer of Novelties, my father is in a position to do the police a few favors, like providing plastic decorations for the Police Ball and other Deserving Charities.

Then my father added, "I've talked to the post office too. They're sure it was posted within the last two days." He'd done favors there too, you see.

As my father said, that Christmas card had all the awful certainty of a letter from the Inland Revenue. We all were quite horribly afraid Aunt Florrie was on her way again.

"But how?" asked my poor father. "I saw her put six foot under. I even lingered to watch the gravediggers shoveling back the earth on top."

"They buried the wrong person," said my mother, trying to convince herself. "A mix-up at the mortuary. I'll bet that son of hers, Albert, was just a big enough twit to keep his eyes shut while he was identifying her corpse."

"It can't have been a lovely sight, at the best of times," said my father. "And after a double-decker bus . . ."

"But where's she been, all this last year? She let Albert sell up her house and furniture and didn't stop him. And that's not like Florrie. . . ."

"Amnesia," announced our Stan, who watches far too many horror videos in the middle of the night when my parents are asleep and they think he is too. "She lost her memory and wanders abroad, a dark, sinister figure in the shadows. . . ."

"If she's lost her memory," said my father, "how come she's remembered about coming here for Christmas Day?"

"She is being drawn by dark forces beyond her control," said Stan.

"I'll give you dark forces," said my mother. "Here you are at twelve o'clock still not washed and dressed, and running around wrapped in your comforter like the Sheikh of Araby. You must've been watching telly since five this morning." Little did she know he'd been up all night.

"All right, then," said our Stan viciously. "She's not lost her memory. She was properly buried, with you watching. So what does that make her? One of the Un-dead, sitting up waiting in the family vault at the cathedral cemetery."

"You mean, she's sitting there writing Christmas cards and waiting to nip out to the post once the sun, which is death to all vampires, sets over the horizon of Liverpool Eight?"

I think my father meant to be sarcastic, get a laugh. In which case he failed. Nobody laughed. Our whole family's so hooked on horror videos, we know more vampires than people. I think they weaken your brain, horror videos.

My mother said, with a nervous giggle, "Well, if she did

suck our blood, she'd only complain about the quality of it." If that was meant to be a joke, that didn't work either.

We didn't do anything else about it, because there was nothing else to do. Except my father didn't invite anybody else around for Christmas Day, just in case.

On Christmas Eve our Stan said, "Don't worry, Dad. She'll have to come in the dark. She'll either be here before seven o'clock in the morning or we'll be okay till teatime."

On that cheering thought we went to bed. But not, for a long time, to sleep. Not me anyway. I heard a dragging sound coming upstairs at half past two and nearly buried my head under my comforter, awaiting the horrid fangs in my neck. But then I heard a young voice say, "Oh, heck," in a most un–Aunt Florrie sort of way. It was Stan, dragging what looked like a small tree upstairs.

"What on earth . . . ?"

"I'm going to cut ash stakes from it. To hammer through her heart."

"What a pity," I said. "It's still got oak galls sticking to it."

I came awake with a horrid jump at half past seven, surprised to find I was still alive. I looked in the mirror, holding my neck to search for fang holes. But there was only the fading love bite that Angela Strang gave me at the third-year party at school, and her intentions were entirely different.

Then I whipped downstairs to the kitchen to make sure Aunt Florrie wasn't sitting there, spilling crumbs of soil all over the new cushion-vinyl and chewing at our cat's neck for starters.

There was no sign of her; just an endless trail of torn Christmas wrapping paper and crumbs all around the house as our Stan raped and pillaged his Christmas presents and helped himself to dates from the lounge and sausage rolls from the kitchen fridge at the same time.

He gave me an evil grin, full of sausage-roll crumbs and date.

"He's come!" he said, only his mouth was so chockablock with sausage roll and date, it came out mushy.

"She's *come?*"

"I said 'He's come.' Santa!"

"I wish you wouldn't speak with your mouth full!"

"We'll be all right till four o'clock now. The sun's shining. Nice bright day. Not a cloud in sight!"

But we did not have a merry day. I couldn't bring myself to care if this year the *Poseidon* sank with all her passengers aboard or not. The Queen's Speech meant as much to me as a goldfish mouthing in a bowl. Stan kept on and on about how she would come.

"Mebbe, quietly, just as a bat, flying through the window like in *Grandson of Nosferatu*. Or mebbe with a chainsaw in both hands, like in *Dracula's Chainsaw Massacre.*"

My mother got up and closed the top window-light, which she'd just opened to let out the near-Russian industrial pollution of my father's chain-smoking.

"That'll not keep her out," said Stan with satisfaction. "Once a vampire's been asked in by somebody in the house, they get in anyway. As a cloud of mist. And we asked her often enough, for Christmas dinner."

The trouble was, she was so much *there* already. The Christmas decorations, the balloons and snow-sprinkled Bambis hanging on the wall, just sort of conjured her up. And I wouldn't have sat on that three-seater all-English-leather Chesterfield to save my life. There was a deep depression in one end, worn there by her huge bottom

on successive Christmases. I sort of couldn't sit there out
of respect for the dead. Or pure panic.

My mother drew the curtains long before daylight
faded. But it wasn't cozy. It just meant we couldn't see
her coming. And I kept remembering her sitting there
from other Christmases, eating her way through boxes of
figs, Turkish Delight. . . . It would take more than figs
and Turkish Delight to satisfy her appetite now.

"I wonder if she *will* fly, like Dracula," said Stan. "If so,
she ought to be here any minute. But she might have to
walk—there aren't many buses running on Christmas
Day—and I bet the undertaker didn't leave any loose
change in her pockets. . . . It could take her hours yet if
she has to walk."

"Would you like a nice, quick, clean death instead, our
Stan?" said my father. "Like me strangling you with a
nice, clean bit of plastic clothesline?"

But nobody laughed. Even Stan stopped gorging himself on the handmade chocolates. There was a marvelous
smell starting to come from the kitchen: roast turkey,
roast potatoes, stuffing. It just made me feel sick.

At twenty past four exactly, at the end of twenty minutes of sweating silence and the sound of my belly rumbling, there came a hammering on our door knocker.

"She's made good time if she's had to walk," said our
Stan.

My dad just sat there paralyzed, puffing on his forty-
second ciggy of the day.

"Shall I let her in, Dad?" asked Stan. "After all, it is
Christmas."

My father tried to answer the door with my mam's cru-
cifix in one hand and her jar of dried garlic from Sainsbury's in the other. He found it quite hard to open the
door with his hands full, and shaking, and sweating. I

kept on thinking she'd made a pretty horrible human being, she'd make a truly appalling vampire.

He got the door open at last. The first thing I noticed was that there was more than one of them, a lot more. I thought wildly that she must have brought some mates from the crypt.

For the creature in the front had her face . . . her green, fishy eyes and stinking fishy breath. Only thinner . . . and all the hair was gone from the top of the head. At least a few straggly strands of hair had been combed across to hide where the skull shone through. And all the little creatures around had her face as well.

And the front figure was wearing feller's trousers and shoes. I thought wildly, a vampire in drag is too much.

I think I screamed before I realized I was going to scream.

"Merry Christmas, Frank," said the creature in a timid, nonvampire voice, grinning. "Don't you recognize me?"

It was her son, Albert. And all his family.

"Come in," my father said. Then he fainted.

"It were like this," said Albert, sitting on the all-English-leather three-seater Chesterfield, with all his family. With a double whiskey in one hand and one of my father's best cigars in the other. "It were like this. After the funeral we had to clear out her house. And we found all her Christmas cards still on the hall table, stamped and ready for posting.

"And our Chrissie here said, 'Waste not, want not,' and brought them home so she could cut off the stamps and reuse them. Only them only being seventeen-pee stamps, we couldn't reuse them till this Christmas, for our own cards. Anyway we'd done our cards one night last week, and it was getting late, so she left our cards on the hall table, with me mother's cards on top, ready to cut the stamps off the next day.

"But silly, bloody little Herbert here thought he'd try and be helpful and took the whole lot down to the postbox at the end of the road and posted them. He can't read yet, you see. He's only seven."

Herbert grinned at me, as if he was really proud of what he'd done.

"Well," continued Albert, "by the time we'd battered out of him what he'd done, it was too late to do anything about it. The last post had gone. So we thought the best thing we could do was to spend Christmas Day going around to all the relations she'd written cards to, explaining what had happened, to put their minds at rest, like.

"And we've had such a day of it! Everyone was that pleased to see us and have it all explained to them. They've been generous, very generous. Sammy offered us all the drinks and mince pies we could sink, and then Henry gave us a really smashing lunch. [Henry has Christmas dinner at lunchtime, 'cause he has to preach somewhere afterward, being a lay preacher.] And then high tea early, at our Tommy's. We were received like the Prodigal Son—the fatted calf wasn't in it. Best Christmas we've had for ages, wi' me laid up wi' me back so much, so I can't work, and nothing for Christmas Day in our house. . . ."

He sniffed at the smell coming from our kitchen, appreciatively. What could my dad do but invite them to stay for Christmas dinner? After they'd been so kind and self-sacrificing?

I can truly say they ate and drank us out of house and home. Dates, nuts, sherry trifle, Babychams, sparkling Asti Spumante, the lot. A proper horde of locusts couldn't have done better.

They didn't go till midnight, after the last bit of Turkish Delight had vanished. And two of the kids were sick on the new wood-block parquet flooring in our hall.

"Well," said Albert between drunken hiccups, "you've made us very welcome, Frank, very welcome indeed. Who would have thought it possible, after all those years of not seeing you." Then he shook Dad's hand on the doorstep, and so did his thin wife, Chrissie, and little Michael and little Herbert, and little Yvonne and little Patrick, and little Olly and little Bernadette with the green icicles hanging off the end of her nose.

"Now that we've started again," Albert added, "we must keep it up. Blood's thicker than water, when all's said and done. See you again next Christmas!"

I don't know about the spirit of Christmas, but I knew then that the spirit of Aunt Florrie would live forever.

As Stan said thoughtfully, "There's more ways than one of being a vampire!"

And that's why, when I've finished helping Dad do his Christmas cards, our whole family is jetting off into the sun, to spend this whole festive season in New Zealand.

I mean, you can't get any farther away, can you?

ROBERT WESTALL

Ghost Abbey, The Scarecrows, The Wind Eye, and *The Devil on the Road* are just a few of Robert Westall's highly praised novels, with *Urn Burial* and *Futuretrack 5* being his most popular novels for young adults. Twice he has been awarded the Carnegie Medal, Britain's highest literary prize; and several of his books have been named Best Books for Young Adults by the American Library Association.

Nearly two thirds of his books have horror/supernatural themes, while several others deal with realistic events from history: *The Machine Gunners,* in which German planes attack a small English town during World War II; *Blitzcat,* an intriguing story about a black cat who follows his master across the English countryside during the Blitz; and *Echoes of War,* five short stories about how war affects individual lives.

His most recent novel, *The Promise,* is a psychological thriller about a beautiful teenage girl who makes her boyfriend promise that if she were ever lost, he would come and find her. Then she dies and becomes a vampire.

With the exception of his cordless telephone and a VCR, Robert Westall prefers things that are old. "I love old churches, old tombstones, old chairs, old clocks," he says. "I even use an old electric typewriter rather than a word processor because words growing on paper are more real to me." He lives in a small town in Cheshire, England.

Mr. Boyle fed his dog more exotic meals than Drew's mother ever fed him. But that wasn't the only unusual thing about Drew's strange neighbor. . . .

THE REINCARNATION OF SWEET LIPS

LARRY BOGRAD

Our wacky neighbor Mr. Boyle sure loved his dog. Personally, though I wished Sweet Lips no harm, I had no use for the spoiled beast. For starters, she enjoyed a stack of toaster waffles for breakfast. Plenty of syrup and rich creamery butter. Then, if she wished, a nap back in her soft, pillowed bed.

I knew this much because I was home for the summer, free from school, bored, and jobless. And my mom's dirt-bag boyfriend, Dale, during his brief run at success as a car salesman, had won a good pair of Japanese binoculars. Plus Mr. Boyle kept his blinds partly opened.

When Mr. Boyle was home, which was all the time it seemed, Sweet Lips was woken from her nap for a stroll around the neighborhood scent points before a satisfying noontime meal. I knew this because some days, when TV and an electric fan made more sense than hanging with my pals all sweaty and looking for trouble, I stayed in. Once home, winded and hungry, Sweet Lips was served ramen noodles with added slices of fresh-cooked lean pork. She dined under a wide umbrella alongside the Boyles' backyard swimming pool. Me, I got by with stiff peanut butter on stale bread, boiling inside our airless house.

One afternoon, at my post behind the front window, I sat and munched—as a fleet of polished sedans pulled up in front of the Boyle place. *Hope they don't disrupt Sweet Lips's long afternoon nap,* I said, yucking, to myself.

Hours later, unbelievably bored (not that I had anything better to do), like four thirty, I watched the sedans refill with men. *Hey, Drew,* I congratulated myself, *way to waste another day of your life.*

That night dinner was a little late next door. Mr. Boyle enjoyed a cocktail or two, while Sweet Lips, up on the kitchen counter, lapped up a bowl of wine. Mom and Dale the Impaler were late, as usual, from their jobs, and I was starving. At least Mom had called, telling me not to worry. But not Dale, because he didn't care.

I would've called out for pizza but didn't want to spend my last cash. Peeking in on the Boyles didn't help. In fact what I saw made me drool like an opened faucet. A choice of microwave entrées for dinner, including fancy lasagna and seafood cooked in Asian sauces. "I wish I was born a dog like Sweet Lips," I said, flopping myself on the couch to watch some old Frankenstein movie on cable.

Approaching 8:00 P.M.—neither Mom nor Dale home, and I too tired to worry—Sweet Lips and Mr. Boyle shared a fudge-covered ice cream bar. Then, about the time I thought of going through the trash to find the sandwich crusts I had thrown away at lunch, Mr. Boyle carried Sweet Lips to the living room, and I heard some relaxing Latin jazz—and I couldn't see to verify, but I'm sure I heard the crunching of popcorn.

Finally, about to devour cardboard smeared with Cheez Whiz, I heard Mom's car pull up. A few moments later she entered behind a shield of bulging grocery sacks.

"It's about time!" I said.

"Drew, don't start. Where's Dale?"

"How should I know?" I asked.

"I called him this afternoon when I knew I'd be home late," Mom explained, restocking the fridge and cupboards. "He promised to pick you up and buy you dinner. He even promised to take you to play miniature golf."

"Haven't seen him," I said, grabbing a peach. "And he didn't call. Mom, when are you going to get rid of that loser?"

"Don't talk about Dale that way," Mom said. But she said this without much conviction. She knew that moving in with Dale had been a planet-size mistake.

I ate the peach and then slam-dunked the pit in the trash. Mom was assembling the dinner selection, freeing items from the plastic sacks. "So how come you had to work so late?" I asked.

"I was meeting with a lawyer," Mom said.

"Mom, you can't divorce Dale until after you marry him," I joked.

"No chance of a wedding, at least not with Dale," Mom said with a sigh. "I needed some legal advice about Dale using my name on a loan. I'm having second thoughts."

"It's about time," I said. "Mom, I'm on my like one-trillionth thought that Dale is a walking toxic site. No offense." Spying a bag of chips, I snatched it before Mom could stop me.

"Don't spoil your appetite," Mom said, being a mom.

"Mom, let's leave Dale in the dust. He's a liar, a loser, and a louse. We're better off alone."

Mom nodded, on the edge of upset. It wasn't that she was above admitting her mistake about Dale. It was figuring how best to leave the scum eater.

At first Dale had seemed too good to be true. He met Mom at a Single and Singular Support Group after his third marriage had broken up. At the time, Mom and Dad had been divorced for years, and she and I were having a pretty good time by ourselves. But she got lonely, especially realizing that in a few more years I'd be out on my own and she'd be alone.

At first Dale did everything right. He made Mom feel wanted and took me to ball games and didn't try to father me. But the instant Mom agreed to move in with him, Dale started showing his true self. Now, six months later, the air turns sour and violent the second he walks in the door and starts giving Mom and me grief. Pardon me, but I wish Dale would disappear and never be found!

"So what's this about a loan?" I asked Mom.

"He convinced me to cosign a loan," she explained. "Right before we moved in together. Said he needed it to pay off his last wife and have her behind him so he could start fresh with me."

"And you believed him?" I asked.

"Drew, I thought I was in love with him!"

"Even so!" Mom was living proof that older is not always wiser.

"Anyway," she said, "he's about to default on the loan. With my name on it I'll be responsible for his unpaid debts. We'll never be totally free of him," she explained.

Keeping busy, fighting back her upset, Mom set about preparing dinner. I eased up on the chips, even rolling up the bag and stashing it on its proper shelf. My next best chance at figuring a plan would come at breakfast.

The next morning, Dale was upstairs sleeping off drink

and his late night. He wasn't due at work until 10:00 A.M. Mom was getting my breakfast out. Last night she'd bought a pint of strawberries, which now graced my cereal. Given another chance, my mom would yet make good. The air was too peaceful to talk of Dale. No, the morning called for a little neighborhood gossip.

"Mom, what is it with Sweet Lips the dog?"

"I suppose that since his wife disappeared, Mr. Boyle has been lonely," Mom said, actually reading Dale's newspaper and enjoying a second cup of coffee. "Dale told me that Mr. Boyle got Sweet Lips as a puppy, right after Wendy, his wife, disappeared."

"His wife disappeared?" What was that about? "His wife disappeared?" I repeated because Mom had said this like this sort of thing happened every day. "What happened to her?"

"She left and hasn't returned," Mom said with a shrug.

"Just like that?" I kept trying.

"I don't know the whole story," Mom said, pushing back her chair. "Time enough to shower and dry my hair and still be at work by eight. Maybe Mrs. Boyle simply ran away from her life," Mom said with wishful thinking. She glanced at me, her loving fifteen-year-old son. "Drew, you're curious about the world. That's a wonderful trait, but it can get you into trouble."

Three hours later, after Dale staggered to his car without breakfast or a hello, I left to mow the lawn for nice and lonely Mrs. Taylor across the street.

"The Boyles, quite a sad story, really," she started, which didn't take much prompting. She was pruning her roses, wearing one of her late husband's shirts, her head under a straw hat. "Rumor has it that Mr. Boyle was involved in some sort of secret research for the government. But whatever he was doing never really worked out."

"Research? What kind of research?"

"Very hush-hush," Mrs. Taylor whispered. "Even Wendy, with whom I shared a book club, whom I considered my friend, wouldn't tell me."

Whatever the research was, maybe it explained the polished sedans yesterday.

"So what do you think happened to Mrs. Boyle?" I asked, stopping to add gas to the mower.

"No idea really," Mrs. Taylor said. "Mr. Boyle was about to go to prison when she disappeared. Then suddenly his legal troubles cleared up."

"Prison?" And here I thought this block was the most boring in the country! "What did Mr. Boyle do?"

Mrs. Taylor took off her hat and wiped her brow with a lacy handkerchief. "What happened happened a few years ago. Nothing was proven one way or the other. And Wendy is now long gone. Sad, sad, sad. If you don't mind, Drew, let's find something else to discuss."

I did a couple rows with the mower. Back and forth, back and forth. Wondering about the Boyles. Scheming how to get rid of Dale. But no inspiration. Then Mrs. Taylor waved her arms and called me over. "Do you smell something foul?"

Certain it was me—it was a hot and sweaty day—I began to apologize. "Mrs. Taylor, it's like ninety degrees and—"

"Oh, no, Drew, I like the smell of a young human body. Of course you're perspiring, it's perfectly natural. Are you sure about not wanting some lemonade?"

Suddenly the smell entered my nostrils. She was right. And it was coming from the Boyles' backyard. Like something had died.

"Oh, I hope Mr. Boyle didn't do something rash," Mrs. Taylor said, worried. "Drew, why don't you just knock at the front door and make sure everything is all right."

"Me? Why me?"

"Because I dare not aggravate my blood pressure problem," Mrs. Taylor said.

Not wanting nice, lonely Mrs. Taylor to croak and leave me without my one summer job, I turned off the mower and headed toward the odor.

I was halfway across the street when I stopped myself from running. What was I doing?!

Still, someone could be hurt or in trouble. So, slowing to a trot to catch my breath, I started again for the Boyles'.

Their front lawn looked awful. More bare dirt than weeds. Much more weeds than patches of dying lawn. The bushes and shrubs had failed to leaf. Suspiciously large ants and flies battled for control of the crumbling cement walk. *Death,* I thought. *This is a death place.* "Anybody home?" I called out, my voice cracking. I wanted my actions public, in case there was trouble.

The smell was intense. Like melting sugar mixed with an overcooked hot dog. "Hello?" I called. "You all right in there? Mr. Boyle? I'm Drew Bonner from next door. Listen, if you hadn't noticed, there's some awful smell coming from your backyard! You burst a pipe or something?!"

To my surprise the door opened. A man appeared wearing an old business jacket over a worn golf shirt and sweatpants. His feet were in flip-flops. "Nice of you to visit, Drew. Please come in," he said in a calmly spooky voice.

"Oh, that's okay, Mr. Boyle. I hate coming into other

people's houses all sweaty. Mrs. Taylor asked me to check on you. Hope I'm not disturbing you."

Beyond him, inside, the drapes were drawn. "Please, I know that we're strangers. I apologize for that. But it would mean a lot to me if you would just come in for a few minutes."

"I'd like to," I lied, "but I have to finish Mrs. Taylor's yard."

Mr. Boyle stepped into the sunlight. Although shaven, his hair was uncombed. "It's Sweet Lips," he announced sadly. "She's gone."

"You lost your dog?" I said, trying to understand.

"No. She's in the backyard. But she's gone."

"Your dog is dead?" I asked, still trying to understand.

Mr. Boyle nodded. "She drowned. It was my fault, really. I should have never thrown that fresh tropical fruit into the shallow end of the pool. It was almost time for our midday dip and snack. By the time I returned in my swimsuit and robe, the fruit must have drifted toward the deep end. Sweet Lips, loving fruit, followed it. Such an awful way to die."

Mr. Boyle was doing his all to fight back tears. He lowered his head and rubbed his temples, needing a moment of private grief.

I felt like an intruder. I turned to leave.

"Drew, please don't leave me," he begged, drawing me back. Taking a moment to compose himself, he then said, "I found Sweet Lips at the bottom of the pool. A large chunk of pineapple wedged between her jaws. I overfed her, but I wanted her happy."

I nodded, wanting nothing more than to make my escape. "Sorry about your pooch," I said, empty-headed.

"Would you be so kind, as long as you're here—there is one favor I would ask of you."

"Sure. Anything," I said without first thinking.

Slightly embarrassed, Mr. Boyle said, "I'm afraid I threw my back out. Would you help me retrieve Sweet Lips's body?"

At first there was no way I was going to dive into some pool to haul some bloated dog corpse to the surface! That was *his* problem!

Then he started offering me money. Fifty dollars. And he was ready to raise himself even higher!

So I cool off and make some bucks by diving for a dead dog, I thought. "Okay, Mr. Boyle," I said, stepping inside.

The front room was ruled by a humongous entertainment center—gigantic column speakers, large-screen TV, audio equipment including individual equalizers for the CD, tuner, and VCR—all built around an enormous refrigerator. No couch or chairs, but big fluffy pillows and plenty of blankets covered with dog hair.

"I had this built for Sweet Lips," Boyle said.

I followed Boyle past the kitchen, where he let me out back through a patio door. The backyard measured no bigger than ours, but it had this big pool bordered by a wide tile deck. No wonder they had never bothered me for lawn service!

Buried in blue water, Sweet Lips looked like a sunken nuclear sub.

"How old was she?" I asked.

"Just four," Boyle said, shaking his head. "Not that old for a dog. She was my life since Wendy left." He attempted a brave smile. "One more thing, Drew. I have a wet suit and mask you should use. The water is quite cold. And I don't want you infected by anything in the water."

"Are you sure I'll be safe? I don't want to catch rabies or something."

"Quite safe," Boyle assured me. "Just make sure that you don't drink any of the pool water."

"Maybe you should get the police," I said, starting to worry.

"Oh, I don't want to involve the police. For your trouble how about I give you five hundred dollars," Mr. Boyle said. "Please. It's important that I bring Sweet Lips inside."

So, on the hottest day of the year I'm geared up like a Navy Seal and dropping, fins first, into Mr. Boyle's pool. Yikes! Even insulated by a wet suit I felt like the water was cold enough to freeze me in seconds!

"Make sure you don't swallow any water," he reminded me. "A little on the skin won't affect you."

Sorry I'd ever been curious in the first place, I inhaled a last breath of warm air, held it, and, shivering, made my approach underwater. The water was absolutely freezing! I had to work fast!

It took some doing—Sweet Lips wet weighed a ton!—but I got the bloated beast out of the drink, a frozen pineapple chunk still trapped in her jaws. Sweet Lips was one wet and stiff and sorrowful sight!

"Thank you. Thank you so much," Mr. Boyle said, covering her with a large, white towel. "I can handle her from here."

I pulled off the scuba mask and wet suit. Wrapped in a towel I rubbed my skin until some feeling returned. Actually it was the easiest five hundred bucks I'd likely ever make. "Happy to help out," I told Mr. Boyle, my teeth still chattering.

"One more thing, Drew," he said, handing me a five-hundred-dollar bill. "I'd appreciate if you don't mention this to anyone. Tell Mrs. Taylor that it was a sewer problem, which I'm taking care of. You understand?"

"Sure, Mr. Boyle," I said. "Whatever you say."

That evening, when Mom got home, I told her about my adventure. Either she wasn't interested or was convinced I'd been on drugs, because she barely raised an eyebrow. Instead she was more concerned about a second secret meeting with a lawyer. "Drew, it's like this. The lawyer thinks we have a fighting chance, but he needs a week to prepare his case. After which we try the courts."

"Dale will kill us first," I said, and she didn't argue.

All she wanted to do after dinner was veg and call her friends for support. Surprising her, I announced a bike ride to the library, something I usually avoided in the summertime.

On a hunch, after asking the reference librarian for help, I looked up "Boyle" in the local newspaper index. Sure enough, there was lots about him like four years ago. Even headlines splashed across the front page for a few days:

HOSPITAL DENIES ILLEGAL RESEARCH

HOSPITAL LAB LOSES U.S. FUNDING

D.A. TO INVESTIGATE RESEARCHER

HOSPITAL BLAMES BOYLE FOR
"CRIMINAL BEHAVIOR"

"MAD SCIENTIST" TRIED TO PLAY GOD

GRAND JURY HEARS CASE AGAINST BOYLE

GRAND JURY DISSOLVED
D.A. BLASTS FED MEDDLING

D.A. LOSES REELECTION
BOYLE CASE BLAMED

SCIENTIST'S WIFE DISAPPEARS

My eyes hurt from too much microfilm reading. But what I'd read was pretty juicy! Wacky Mr. Boyle claimed he could "transform life!" That he had discovered the "secret of spontaneous generation!" Editorials labeled him a "dangerous quack" and "Frankensteinish." Wow! I'd never lived next door to a scientist before. Much less a mad scientist!

The library was about to close. I thanked the librarian and rode my bike home. Unfortunately, when I walked in Dale and Mom were having a horrible fight. I was used to them screaming at each other lately—but tonight something much worse had happened.

Mom was rubbing her face. Her eyes and cheeks wet. "Hello, Drew," she said quietly.

"What's going on here?" I demanded.

"Go to your room!" Dale warned me.

"Hey, you're not my father!" I told him. "You're not even my stepfather."

"Go to your room!" he demanded.

"Or what?" I shot back. "You'll hit me like you hit my mom? If you ever, ever lay a finger on her again, I'll—"

"You'll what?" Dale sneered. He picked up his car keys and stopped by the door, elbowing me out of his way. "You cosigned that loan legally," he told Mom. "Some lawyer can't help you. If you and Drew want to move out, fine. I'll help you pack. But your money is mine. You'll never be rid of me!" With that he left. In a moment we heard his car racing down the block.

"Are you all right?" I asked Mom.

She nodded. "I need a shower. Oh, Drew, I really made a mess of things, didn't I?"

I didn't answer her. She'd had a rough night without me rubbing it in. But later, when I went to my room, I decided that no matter what it took, I was going to rid us of Dale once and for all!

Later, at what exact time I don't know, a smell woke me. A pleasant, hopeful smell. Not unlike sniffing a bouquet of roses. Led by my nostrils, I followed the smell toward the window. Whatever it was, it was coming from the Boyle house.

Curious, I threw on some clothes and sneaked out back. Mr. Boyle had closed the drapes, so no peeking through the front or side windows. But, boy, was that smell strong, bringing with it the promise of spring!

Checking that no one was watching, I jumped the fence, then walked around the Boyles' pool, toward the kitchen window. My pulse throbbing, I crouched low and kept out of sight.

At first I didn't dare look, but what I heard sounded like something trying to be born! Slurping and sliding! Straining and ripping! If it hadn't been for that pleasant smell, I would've thrown up for sure!

"That's it, darling!" I heard Mr. Boyle shout. "Keep pushing! You're almost free!"

A sensible person would've raced home and called the cops. Instead I quietly carried over a chaise longue, placed it under the window, and climbed up for a look.

What?! I shook my head, refocusing my vision. It can't be! Was I dreaming?!

Spread on a large plastic sheet in the living room I saw —what?—*something* struggling to free itself from Sweet Lips's dead body! Bones cracking! Blood spurting! The thing twisting! Grunts about to explode into screams! My chin dropped against my chest. I had to reach down with my hand and push my jaws together.

Skin and fur and muscle tore! My cheeks puffed, and I covered my mouth. *Run, you idiot!* I thought, but my legs were locked, unable to run from the horror I watched. The poor corpse of Sweet Lips was being wrecked from inside!

"One more push!" Mr. Boyle encouraged. "Don't give up now!"

My forehead pressed against the windowpane, my eyes wide as basketballs, I watched in shock and wonder as—a naked woman arose from the hapless shell of Sweet Lips the dog!

I tried to scream but couldn't find the air to force out the sound.

Wiping fur and blood from her mouth, the woman looked at Mr. Boyle and said, "Just look at me! I'll have to diet for months and months."

"Wendy, darling, you look beautiful," Boyle said, embracing the slimy woman and then offering her a terrycloth robe. "Sorry about the excess pounds, but I wanted to do something to show you that I cared. Welcome home, Wendy!"

Wendy? Boyle's disappeared wife?

This was all too much! Trying to get away, I caught a foot in the chaise and went crashing to the ground. Before I could free myself and escape, Mr. and Mrs. Boyle were standing above me!

"Wendy, our neighbor, Drew Bonner," Mr. Boyle said calmly. "He's the lad who pulled you from the pool."

"Please overlook my appearance," Mrs. Boyle said. Using her fingers, she was cleaning gunk from her hair.

In reply I stammered a high-pitched "Pleased to meet you."

"If you'll excuse me," Mrs. Boyle said, "I'd like to clean up and find an outfit I can fit into. Nice to meet you, Drew."

Mr. Boyle helped me to my feet. "Now, Drew, you know the old saying, 'Curiosity killed the cat.' "

"Are you going to kill me?!"

"Of course not," Mr. Boyle assured me. "But what you saw must remain a secret."

"Your wife is Sweet Lips. Or rather she *was* Sweet Lips. Or Sweet Lips is your wife. Or Sweet Lips was your wife. Right?" I stammered, never feeling so weird in my life.

"For a while the government was very interested in my research," Mr. Boyle explained, taking me inside for a bowl of ice cream and some cookies. "Of course, after the hospital found out the true nature of my research, all trouble broke loose. All my notebooks and equipment were taken. If the CIA hadn't intervened, which took some doing, poor Wendy might have remained a canine forever."

"So that's what those sedans were. Yesterday," I said. "You're working for the CIA!"

"Actually no," Mr. Boyle said. "Oh, I realized that a few months ago I had finally achieved a breakthrough. Stupidly I called the spooks, since they had paid for my new research. Luckily, though, by the time they arrived, I realized I didn't want the government to have my formula. Imagine what mischief they would get into! So I purposely cooled the solution until it left Wendy—Sweet Lips—in suspended animation."

"But the water or whatever was so cold that she remained in this frozen state," I said. "That is, until I pulled her to the surface so you could revive her."

"Quite right," Boyle said. "Drew, you have the makings of a real scientist!"

I finished my ice cream and cookies. Wendy Boyle, wearing some sort of muumuu, came in to wish me a good night. Having been turned from a dog back into a woman had been very tiring, and she was heading for bed.

"So the solution in the pool is what turned Wendy into Sweet Lips in the first place," I said to Mr. Boyle.

He nodded. "The D.A. was closing in on me. Wendy, being a loving and loyal wife, convinced me to try the solution on her before it was lost forever. Oh, it worked. But it's taken me four long years to reconstruct my research and return my Wendy to me. Another scoop of chocolate chocolate chip?"

"No, thank you," I said. "So that's why you wanted me to be careful in the pool," I observed.

"Precisely," Mr. Boyle said. "Promise me you'll keep our secret."

"Don't worry, Mr. Boyle," I said. "The secret is safe with me."

"Well, in that case, I'll see you to the door."

"Actually it's best if I jump the fence and get back into my house through the back door," I said. I rubbed my throat. "All this excitement. My throat is really dry. Could I get a glass of water to go?"

"Of course." Mr. Boyle pulled down a paper cup from a dispenser near the sink. He filled the cup with water and handed it to me. "There you go."

He walked me out the back. "Tomorrow morning I drain the pool for good," he said. He seemed half-sad, half-glad.

"And lose your solution forever?" I asked.

"I have Wendy back. That's what is important," he said. "I don't want to risk any more trouble. Well, good night, Drew."

"Good night, Mr. Boyle," I said. "And thanks."

"For the ice cream?"

"For the ice cream and a totally bizarre time," I said.

He waited until I headed for the fence. I stopped only to drink the water from the paper cup. Then I crumpled the cup and put it in my pocket, not to be a litterbug. As I started to climb the fence, I looked back and saw Mr. Boyle going inside and turning off the lights.

Carefully I lowered myself to the ground, still inside the Boyles' backyard. After a few minutes, certain that no one was watching, I took the crumpled cup and straightened it out. Then I crept to the pool and—without getting my hand wet—filled the cup with the secret solution.

"There," I whispered to myself. "Here's your morning coffee, Dale!"

The five hundred dollars that Mr. Boyle had given me to rescue Sweet Lips went toward the deposit on a new apartment when Mom and I moved a few weeks later. Suddenly free of Dale, we wanted a new start in a new place. Of course we had to find an apartment that would take pets.

Because the morning that Dale apparently took off, this stray mutt wandered into our lives for good.

LARRY BOGRAD

Larry Bograd wrote his first novel when he was nineteen, but it wasn't until several years later—when he was managing editor at Harvey House Publishers—that he started writing for children and young adults. After *Felix in the Attic* and two other illustrated books, he published *The Kolokol Papers,* the first of his five novels for young adults. Set in Russia, it describes a teenage boy's efforts to publicize his family's oppressed life in Moscow and the KGB's arrest of his human-rights-activist father.

Born in Denver, Colorado, Bograd's love of the American West is reflected in both *Los Alamos Light* and *Travelers.* In the latter story a seventeen-year-old boy searches for answers about his father's death in the Vietnam War. Bograd's own experiences provided some of the background for that book as well as his other novels. *The Better Angel,* about a teenage love triangle, is partly based on his own senior year in high school, he says. And *Bad Apple* resulted from his experiences working at a shelter for runaways in the Times Square area of New York City.

Larry Bograd lives in Denver, where he is an assistant professor of English at Metropolitan State College of Denver and, with his wife, Coleen Hubbard, runs Writers Lab, a theatrical company committed to new works.

When he was alive, Finlay was a faithful and protective dog. In death he's even more so. . . .

A NASTY, MUDDY GHOST DOG

JOAN AIKEN

We have a ghost dog in our family. Or we did, at least, until Grandma came to live with us. Then the trouble began.

The dog's name is Finlay. When Finlay was alive, he was a ginger-biscuit-colored bullterrier. He was very gentle with small children. They could do anything to him: thump him and roll on him and tickle him, and he loved it. He also loved food. He hated all other dogs, visitors, salespeople, mail carriers, and meter readers, and would chase them for miles if given the chance. And he could run faster than a greyhound. My brother Greg used to exercise Finlay on his bike, pedaling flat out, and even then Finlay was always ahead.

So it was a big relief to some people, especially the mail carrier, when Finlay got knocked over by a brewers' truck one day as he rushed out of our front gate and across the road after a spaniel that was walking along, minding its own business.

We buried him sadly in the back garden with a big wreath of dog violets and dogwood and supposed that would be the last of him.

But we were wrong. Because we soon began to hear his ghost around the house: toenails scratching up and down the stairs, heavy breathing and whines in the kitchen when tins were opened or meat cut up, loud barking when the doorbell rang, and furious growls when somebody opened the gate.

Only two people could actually *feel* Finlay. One was Grandma, who came to live with us shortly after he died.

"Lucky it wasn't while he was alive," said Dad.

Alive or dead, it didn't seem to make much difference. Finlay, when not chasing anyone, liked to lie pressed close against the solid-fuel stove in the kitchen, on the warm hearthstone. Grandma couldn't see him there, but she kept tripping over him when she went to put on a kettle. This made her cross. It was dangerous, she said.

"You've got to get rid of that dog," she said.

"How?" said Dad. "Just tell me, how?"

The other person who could feel Finlay was my brother Daniel, aged five.

When he was alive, Finlay always used to sneak up and spend the night on Dan's bed, if Ma didn't find out and stop him. And—of course—now that he was a ghost, Ma *couldn't* stop Finlay. Dan loved Finlay's company. They had agreed that Finlay could stretch across the whole bed and Dan would sleep in a loop of blanket dangling down the side.

Another thing Finlay had been keen on when he was alive was the sound of my brother Greg playing the organ.

Music is Greg's main thing. He plays the piano and violin, and he found this little old pedal organ in a junkyard and bought it for ten pounds and worked on it for months, repairing it. Now it's in our front room, and Greg had the habit of playing it after supper while Ma wrote letters and Dad read the paper.

Greg's organ playing used to send Finlay crazy with joy:

wherever he was (mostly, at that time, it would be on Dan's bed), he'd throw up his head and let out long, breathy, sobbing, boo-hooing howls of rapture—"Oh, woo-hoo-hoo-hoo! Oh, ow, wow, wow-wow-woo-hoo-hoo!" —which could be heard all down our street and as far away as the pharmacist's on the corner.

Daniel loves our brother Greg's playing too. Especially one tune. The twiddle tune, he calls it. "Play the twiddle tune tonight, Greg," he'd say, going upstairs, and so Greg usually ended with that. It has a lot of twiddles, as you'd guess.

When Dan was a bit smaller, he used to be scared of going to bed for some reason; didn't like going up to his room and leaving us all on the floor below. But Greg's music and Finlay's company quite put an end to that; Dan would skip up the stairs and lie happy as a dormouse, with Finlay hollering away beside him and the sound of the organ coming up from below.

But Grandma put a stop to all that.

She couldn't stand organ music, she said, it was absolutely her least favorite noise. "*Don't* ever play that thing while I'm in the house, *if* you please," she said. "I simply cannot endure it. Let alone the disgusting sound of that animal howling!"

The trouble was that Grandma always was in the house, never out of it, except every third Tuesday evening, when she went to her bridge club. So Dan and Finlay had to manage without their go-to-bed music.

"It isn't fair," Dan said night after night.

Grandma wasn't even satisfied with having stopped the music; she wanted to get rid of Finlay altogether. Even his ghost. She went on and on about it.

"I don't care what you say, it's not decent," she said. "Having a ghost dog about the house, grunting and scratching at fleas you can't see, and growling at the vicar when he comes to call. I don't see why I should stand for it.''

"And what do you suggest we do?" snapped Ma, who had been fond of Finlay.

Surprisingly Grandma produced an idea that seemed quite practical.

"Why don't you take him back to where he came from?" she said.

Where Finlay had come from was a farm in Suffolk that bred bullterriers.

"I suppose it might work," Dad said doubtfully. "If the old boy went back to where he was a pup . . . I suppose he might *like* to go back."

"There'd be plenty of others for him to fight," remarked Greg. "He'd like that."

None of us really cared for the idea, but in the end Grandma had her way. She usually did, because she was ready to go on arguing longer than anybody else. And Dad said (when she was up in her bedroom), "After all, she *is* a poor old lady who can't afford a place of her own."

Taking Finlay to Suffolk was no problem. For always, as soon as the car was parked out in front, he'd be there, ready to bound in as soon as the rear door was opened and stand on the backseat with his forepaws on either side of the driver's headrest, mouth open, tongue all the way out, staring ahead through the windscreen as if he were on the watch for snipers.

"So who's coming with me?" said Dad, rather sadly.

Ma said she'd stay with Grandma; Greg had a music exam; so Dan and I went. We sat on either side of Finlay in the back while Dad drove around the M25. Dan had his arm around Finlay, and even I thought that I could feel his warm, solid shoulder against mine. When he was alive, Dad said, Finlay was as heavy as a barrel of nails.

After about an hour, when we had left the motorway, Dad stopped at a wayside garage for petrol. Now we were getting quite close to Finlay's birthplace, and we had all three gone silent. But Finlay seemed very interested in the landscape, and we could hear him sniffing, as if the air was telling him something.

This was where we had our adventure.

Dad had got out of the car (it was a self-service place) and Finlay had flumped back on the seat between Dan and me, and we were leaning against him.

All of a sudden two men in stocking masks came running, pushing Dad ahead of them (he looked startled to death), pulled open the door, shoved Dad into the driving seat, and bundled in beside him in front.

"Now, drive—fast!" said one man. "We'll tell you where. Come on—start the motor!"

He glanced behind him, saw Dan and me, plainly reckoned we weren't worth bothering about, just a couple of kids, and dumped a heavy case he was carrying between us. It landed right on top of Finlay, who growled.

That surprised the man. He said, "What the—" and peered about, saw nothing, poked Dad in the ribs with something he held (later we heard it was a gun), and said, "Get on with it! *Drive!*"

So Dad started the motor and pulled out onto the road.

That was when things really broke loose.

It was plain that Finlay hadn't liked having a case dumped on him; and of course he always hated strangers at any time. Now he let out a really bloodcurdling growl and a whole hurricane of angry barks and launched himself forward like a missile.

Dan said afterward that he had heard Finlay's jaws snap together.

The man next to Dad let out a shattering yell.

"Ahhhhh! Get it *off* me!" he screamed.

Then the man beyond him gave a yell, too, and panicked, opening the left-hand door and hurling himself into the road. Lucky for him, the car was not yet moving very fast; he fell and rolled over, then picked himself up and began to run. His mate followed, still screaming, clutching at the back of his neck as if he felt teeth digging into his spine.

Dan and I felt Finlay catapult himself over the seat back and out through the open door after the men. We could see them scudding down the road. One swerved into the path of an oncoming motorcyclist. The other tripped and fell into the ditch.

Now a police car came shooting up behind us, hee-hawing away, blue lights ablaze. A clump of cops tumbled out of it and soon had the two masked men quelled and handcuffed. (One of them had his leg broken anyway.)

We learned they had stolen a valuable painting from Frame Court, a big house nearby, and the police had already been after them when they stopped at the garage to swap cars.

"It certainly was their bad luck that you had such a well-trained guard dog with you," one of the cops told Dad respectfully. "Where has he got to?" they asked, glancing around.

"Oh, he probably got overexcited and ran off into the fields," Dad said casually. "He'll turn up by and by."

In fact, although we called and whistled, Finlay didn't come back. Perhaps, we thought sadly, he really *was* happy to be back in his old haunts.

*   *   *

The house, when we got home, seemed dreadfully quiet without him.

Of course Grandma was delighted.

"You see! I was quite right!" said she.

Before we heard any news of Finlay, we had a surprise. It seemed there was a reward of ten thousand pounds from Lord Frame for the return of the stolen painting, which was a very valuable one, of a bullterrier, by a painter named Landseer.

"No *wonder* Finlay didn't like having it dumped on him!" said Dan.

Dad was to get the money, though he kept saying, "Really I didn't do anything." But they told him that, since he had trained his fine dog to pounce on the thieves, the reward was rightfully his. In the end he stopped arguing and took the money and gave it to Grandma as a down payment for a nice flat in the middle of town, where she could see her friends and be much more comfortable than she was in our house.

"Though really I'm quite all right here," she said when he first suggested it, "now that that nasty beast has left. Really I'm quite happy."

We weren't very happy. In fact we were pretty miserable, and my brother Dan was just about heartbroken. He had big black circles under his eyes, and he simply hated going to bed at night.

But after five days Finlay turned up. There was a howl outside the front door one evening, and Dan rushed to open it.

"He must have been fighting all the way from *there* to *here*," Dan said, hugging the invisible Finlay, hugging and hugging, and feeling him all over. "He's covered in bites and absolutely caked in mud. He must have swum about forty rivers!"

The only thing Finlay wanted was to lie down on Dan's bed.

"Honestly!" said Grandma. "The sooner I'm out of this unhygienic house, the better. To let a nasty, muddy ghost of a dog lie on that boy's *bed*! Why, you don't know where he's *been*!"

But even Ma wouldn't have dreamed, just then, of trying to stop Finlay. He and Dan went upstairs together, arm around neck. And Greg played all Dan's favorite pieces on the organ, ending with the twiddle tune; and Finlay stretched out, wider and wider, over the whole of Dan's bed, moaning and howling, horribly out of tune with the music:

"Oh, woo-hoo, hoo-hoo-hoo! Oh, ow, wow-wow, woo-hoo-hoo-hoo-hoo!"

JOAN AIKEN

British by birth, though the daughter of a famous American poet, Joan Aiken has published more than eighty books, about two thirds of them for young people. About half of her books are devoted to fantasy/supernatural topics, most recently a collection of ghost stories entitled *Give Yourself a Fright.* Although she is very much interested in ghosts, she says she has never met one herself, even though she has lived in two houses that are reputed to be haunted.

Among her best-known novels are *The Wolves of Willoughby Chase,* published in 1962, for which she won the Guardian Award for children's literature, and *Midnight Is a Place,* a Dickens-like story about an orphaned boy and the exploitation of child labor in mid-nineteenth-century England. Her focus on the nineteenth century and industrialization is also evident in her most recent novel, *Is.*

She is also working on a new novel for adults about Lamb House, the famous home of author Henry James in Rye, Sussex, England, where writer E. F. Benson also lived and saw a ghost.

But the fantasy short story is the literary form that Joan Aiken enjoys writing most. Among her collected works are *A Touch of Chill, A Whisper in the Night,* and *Arabel's Raven.* Writing short stories, she says, "comes closest to free flight."

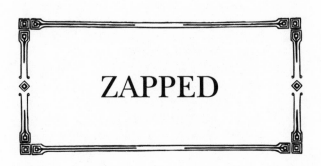

ZAPPED

Buck sold encyclopedias door to door. But he should have read the fine print before he knocked at Mr. Gordon's house. . . .

SALESMAN, BEWARE!

STEVEN OTFINOSKI

Interplanetary teenage salesman #19908 Buck Smith stopped short at the iron gate before the modest, split-level house at the end of Green Moon Drive. There, posted on the railing, was a small plastic sign with bold red lettering on a cream background that read:

BEWARE OF THE OOMELECK!

"Oomeleck," muttered Buck under his breath. "What in the Milky Way is an oomeleck?"

The tall, fair-haired youth lowered his bulky sample case to the gravel walkway, reached into a zippered pocket on his antigravitational space suit, and pulled out a small white card. The card had been issued by the Universal Encyclopedia Company, for which Buck worked during the summer months. It identified dangerous pets to be avoided on the particular planet where he happened to be peddling his wares—in this case, Saturn.

Buck read aloud as he ran his finger down the list of resident beasts. " '*Noodleburr:* a five-legged cat with razor-sharp claws. . . . *Qaggledorf:* a creature resembling a cross between a rhinoceros and an alligator; has a particularly nasty disposition. . . .' "

An oomeleck, whatever it was, did not make the list. Buck Smith looked at the sign a second time and tapped his metallic space shoe on the azure-colored gravel. A less persistent salesman would have hopped into his solar-powered space scooter and headed for the next block, but Buck, despite his youth, was made of sterner stuff. Besides, the long Saturn day was drawing to a close, and he needed only one more sale to win that little two-seater starmobile the main office was awarding to the salesperson with the highest monthly sales quota.

It occurred to Buck that the sign could be an empty threat devised by a disgruntled Saturnite to discourage door-to-door salespersons. He had run into this type of customer many times before. After a little high-powered sales pitch, their resistance often crumbled away. Some of them, in fact, proved to be among his best customers. Buck gritted his teeth and swung open the unlocked gate.

Despite his outward bravado he could feel his heart pounding fiercely as he walked the dozen steps to the front door. But no mysterious shaggy-haired creature leaped out of the thick bushes and sank its sharp teeth into his leg. He breathed a sigh of relief and pressed the sonar buzzer twice. Silence.

Still slightly nervous, Buck suddenly remembered that the sample volume in his case covered the letters *N–O*. He put down his case and took out the green-covered book. But before he could look up *oomeleck,* he heard the pad of heavy footsteps and quickly put the heavy tome back in his case. The door opened a crack, and a middle-aged gentleman with a sagging belly and a balding head peered curiously out at him.

"Yes?" asked the homeowner with no trace of hostility.

"Good day, sir," replied Buck, flashing his best salesman smile. "Pardon me if I seem a little surprised, but I wasn't sure how welcome I'd be after reading your sign out front."

The man looked puzzled for a second and then gave out with a sharp laugh.

"Oh, *that,*" he said. "I should've taken that sign down months ago. The former owner put it up to keep away strangers. He was a most unsociable person."

"Oh," said Buck, his confidence returning. "Let me introduce myself. My name is Buck Smith and I'm working my way through Earth U., North American campus, selling encyclopedias. Perhaps you've heard of my employer, the Universal Encyclopedia Company. 'If it's in the universe, it's in Universal.' "

The man stared blankly at Buck.

"That's, er, our slogan," explained the salesman. "Tell me, Mister . . ."

"Gordon," came the reply.

"Tell me, Mr. Gordon, do you own an encyclopedia?"

"No," said Mr. Gordon, shaking his head slightly. "Frankly I don't read much."

"All the more reason for you to own the twenty-two-twenty edition of the Universal Encyclopedia," said Buck, the words tripping off his tongue. "It's written in clear, concise language that could save you years of needless reading through dozens of other reference books. If you could spare me just a few precious moments of your time, I could tell you why I feel this encyclopedia would be an indispensable addition to your home library."

"Well, all right," said the lumpy man somewhat reluctantly. "Come in, Mr. Smith."

Buck stepped into the small living room and took a seat on a large, inflated plastic couch. As he delivered his pitch, he took out the sample volume once more. A sudden gleam came into Mr. Gordon's small, sluggish eyes at the sight of the finely tooled emerald cover.

"May I?" he asked politely, extending a fleshy hand toward the book.

"Certainly. Browse through it."

The man ran his thick, clumsy fingers almost reverently over the smooth, gold-edged binding and the embossed cover. Buck could already picture himself zipping around the ionosphere on that snappy little starmobile.

"That's genuine Venusian lizard skin," pointed out the salesman. "It's guaranteed to never wear out."

Mr. Gordon gave a perfunctory flip of the pages.

"If you buy a set now," continued Buck, "you'll not only receive an amazing discount but also get—at no extra cost—a special how-to book that helps you complete hundreds of home projects, from building your own family-size rocket to starting your own space colony on a dead planet."

"How much is a set?" asked the customer.

The directness of the question took the salesman aback.

"Only fifty thousand, two hundred ninety-two intergalactic dollars," he replied, regaining his momentum. "Of course, with our special layaway plan it can cost you as little as five hundred ninety-five dollars a lunar month for a period of—"

"I'll take a set," interrupted the man, snapping the book shut.

For the first time in his rising career Buck Smith was at a complete loss for words. "Don't you want to hear about some of the other special features first?" he finally managed to sputter.

"That won't be necessary, young man," smiled Mr. Gordon. "You're a most persuasive salesman."

Buck would have been quick to agree, except that he had hardly had the opportunity to show off his stuff.

"Do you have more volumes with you?" asked the man. "In the lizard skin, that is?"

"Well, no," replied the salesman. "But I assure you, you'll receive your full twenty-eight-volume set within thirty days."

"Then I'll take this volume for now until the others arrive," said Mr. Gordon quickly, clutching the green book in both hands.

Buck was about to object, but then remembered the shiny new starmobile. "Uh, this is a little irregular," he said, "but if you'd like to keep the sample, I think I can let you have it until your full set arrives."

"Thank you, young man," said the grateful customer. And Buck could have sworn there were tears welling in the man's tiny, piggish eyes.

"I have the contract right here for your signature," said Buck, whisking some papers from his case. Mr. Gordon took the pen offered him and scribbled his name on the dotted line, without reading a word of the fine print.

For the second time that day Buck Smith was speechless. "And how would you like to pay for your set?" he asked at last.

"Oh, cash, of course" was the brisk reply.

Buck had to repress a gasp. He hadn't had a customer pay in cash in the three summers he'd been working for Universal.

"Is that all right?" asked the man, noticing Buck's reaction.

"Perfectly all right, Mr. Gordon," the salesman managed to get out.

Just then the interplanetary telecommunicator in the next room gave off a series of annoying bleeps.

"Excuse me for a moment, please," said the man, rising from his chair. He lumbered off down the hall as Buck leaned back on the couch and smiled. The other boys back at the office on Earth weren't going to believe this one, he thought. But Buck's pleasure was mixed with a vague dissatisfaction at how easy it had been. Buck was one of the best summer salesmen in the solar system. His manager boasted he could sell an icebox to a Plutonian. This Saturnite had not offered the slightest sales resistance to test his mettle. There was something almost unsportsmanlike about it.

As he waited for the customer's return, Buck glanced down at the sample volume on the coffee table and remembered once more the sign on the gate. With mild curiosity he opened the book and flipped through the pages. He paused at the brief entry he had been searching for on page 1,091 and began to read. As he finished, his eyes narrowed, and a vague uneasiness came over him.

Suddenly he heard strange noises coming from the other room. There was a loud wheezing, like the heavy breathing of some ungainly animal or a monstrous machine.

Buck tried to get a grip on his imagination, triggered by what he had just read. He shut the book and called out in as firm a voice as he could muster, "Is everything all right, Mr. Gordon?"

The only reply was a terrible, unearthly roar as Buck Smith gasped in horror at the thing that came toward him through the hall. . . .

* * *

The oomeleck gave a small belch of satisfaction and stretched its three-thousand-pound pink body on the living room floor. Those lizard skin covers had been a gourmet's dream. The pages between them had been less tasty, but filling. The creature stuck a long purple claw into its gargantuan mouth and deftly removed a piece of grist—the last vestige of interplanetary salesman #19908 —from between two large incisors. Buck had been meaty, but he couldn't compare in flavor with his product.

The oomeleck, whose name was in fact Rex, uttered a long sigh as he thought of the young, cheerful salesman. He almost regretted having to devour him. He had enjoyed his company and rarely had the opportunity to converse with anyone other than his ill-tempered master, the real Ralph Gordon.

However, the phone call had been from Gordon himself, telling his pet he would be home shortly. Rex knew his master would be furious if he found him entertaining another salesman while he was at work. Rex had to destroy all the evidence at once, including the salesman. He shivered to think what Gordon would do if he found he had been eating in the living room again. Probably give him another spanking with that dreadful rolled newspaper.

He picked up the contract from the floor where Buck had dropped it and chewed it sadly. There was no chance that Gordon would accept the books, even if he mailed the contract to Universal himself. His master, alas, did not share Rex's enthusiasm for the written word or Venusian lizard skin.

But in his haste to tidy up the room, the oomeleck failed to notice some of the torn pages from the sample volume that he had dropped in his eating frenzy. If he had, he might have been amused by the encyclopedist's description of himself—the last thing that Buck Smith had ever read:

OOMELECK—A rare creature native to the planet Saturn. Oomelecks are large, voracious animals that will eat almost anything. The most striking characteristic of these highly dangerous beasts is their ability to change their entire molecular structure at will.

STEVEN OTFINOSKI

After working for a year as a newspaper reporter, Steven Otfinoski was determined to be a free-lance writer. But his early efforts were fruitless until he landed a job in the mailroom of Xerox Educational Publications, home of *My Weekly Reader,* in his hometown of Middletown, Connecticut. He worked his way up to assistant editor of *Read* magazine and then was laid off. Since that fateful occasion, Steve has published over forty books for young people and has written a number of plays and children's musicals, many of which have been performed in regional theaters and Off-Off Broadway. During the summer of 1991 one of his plays was even performed at Stratford-upon-Avon, England.

Most of his recent publications have been nonfiction, including *Hispanics in American History, 1865 to the Present; Nineteenth-Century Writers*—short biographies of ten American literary giants, from Washington Irving to Stephen Crane; and *Nelson Mandela: The Fight Against Apartheid.*

But Otfinoski also enjoys writing horror/mystery/adventure stories for young adults, incorporating humor where many other writers use gore. Among his most popular novels are *The Screaming Grave* and *The Shrieking Skull.*

Steve and his wife, also a free-lance writer as well as a harpist, live in Stratford, Connecticut, with their two children, Daniel and Martha.

Like father, like son, goes the old saying. But Sue Ellen acts as if Zach is his father . . . ?

SOMETHING'S DIFFERENT

FRANCES A. MILLER

The first time I saw her, I didn't think anything of it. I was bicycling home after a varsity baseball game—my first shutout of the year—and replaying the highlights in my mind so I could share them with Dad at supper like we always did. As I turned down our dirt road, I caught a glimpse of movement in the doorway of the old Mennart place.

Nobody's lived there since before I was born, so I slowed up a little, thinking it might be kids fooling around. The place is supposed to be haunted, and kids dare each other to go inside, but the floor is rotten and the whole place is falling in. Dad and I chase kids out of there all the time. We're scared that someday the house is going to come down on one of them.

At first I couldn't tell who it was. My eyes were kind of blurry, and I had to rub them a couple of times before I saw her clearly. It was a girl, about eighteen or nineteen. She was standing in the doorway, watching me ride past —really staring, her body rigid and tense. It made me uncomfortable, so I poured it on for the last half mile, yelling for my dog, Strider, as I skidded expertly to a stop beside our back porch.

Dad was out on the tractor, mowing the hay in the

front pasture. From the look of it, he was going to be out there for another hour or two. By the time I'd taken care of the animals, showered, done my homework, and gotten supper going, I'd forgotten about the girl.

I saw her twice the next day. In the morning she was sitting on the porch steps as if she'd spent the night there. I knew Dad wouldn't like that. He hated that dying old place, but he wouldn't want some careless camper burning it down and setting our fields on fire. If she was still there that afternoon, I figured I'd better tell him.

She was still there, leaning on the corner where the fences joined, so I had to pass real close as I turned into our road. I couldn't pretend I didn't see her, so I stopped.

She smiled at me, kind of a slow, sexy smile. *Whoa, I* thought. *You've got the wrong guy, lady.* I smiled back, but I could feel myself blushing. Dad is the ladies' man in our family. He started going out again after Mom left us, and he still goes out more than I do.

"You buying the Mennart place?" I said. She didn't answer, just went on smiling like she hadn't heard me. *Maybe she's deaf,* I thought. "Well, I gotta get going," I said. "Watch out for the floors in there." *You're a real helpful guy, Zach,* I told myself as I pedaled furiously up the road. Warning a woman who can't hear you about a rotten floor.

"Hey, Dad," I said at supper. "Did you see the girl at the Mennart place today? Are they finally going to sell it?" I was really freaked by Dad's reaction.

He jerked as if I'd kicked him. The spoonful of chili on its way to his mouth went flying. I could hear Strider gobbling it up as I stared at Dad's face. Under the tan his skin was greenish gray.

"What girl?" he said hoarsely.

"The girl down at the Mennart place. She was there yesterday too. You didn't see her?" How could he have missed her? He'd been haying all day in the pasture across the road from their place.

"What did she look like?" He still hadn't moved. He was staring at me as if he were trying to see inside my head.

"She's blond, about eighteen, kind of small, sexy smi—"

Shifting from paralyzed into high gear, Dad was out the back door while I was still talking. His chair smacking against the wall and the slam of the screen got me going too. I sprinted down the road after him.

"What's up?" I said breathlessly as I caught up to him. He was half running himself.

"Wait," he said. "I'll tell you later . . . if I have to."

We stopped where we had a clear view of the Mennart place. She was in the backyard, wandering aimlessly around in the waist-high weeds. I waited for Dad to say something, but he just scrutinized the place inch by inch as if he were looking for someone in a crowd and not finding her.

"There she is," I said impatiently. He would have been blind not to see her.

He turned on me. "Where?"

"Right there," I said. "In the backyard." I didn't like this game we were playing. It gave me the creeps. "Dad . . . come on."

He stared at the yard, but I could tell he wasn't seeing her. "Dad . . . ?" My voice came out high and squeaky, like I was five years old again and scared of the dark. Dad came back from wherever he'd gone and looked at me as if he wasn't sure who I was. Then he slung an arm across my shoulders, gave me a rough, reassuring hug, and we headed home. When I glanced back, she was leaning on the fence watching us go. Behind her, half hidden in the black rectangle of the open door, someone else was watching too.

As soon as we were inside our house, Dad shut the door and locked it. That really spooked me. Even though we're the only ones on that stretch of road, I'd never been scared of being alone . . . until now. He picked up his chair and made a gesture that meant I should sit too. When we were staring at each other across the table, he started in.

"How much do you know about the Mennart place?"

"Just what I've heard from the kids at school. The last guy who lived there killed his wife, and when the sheriff came for him, they had a big shoot-out, and he was killed. And nobody's lived there since."

"What I'm going to tell you, Zach, stays right here. Okay?"

"Okay," I said. What I really wanted was for him to drop the whole thing.

"It happened when I was your age. They moved in just about this time of the year. Gene his name was, and hers was Sue Ellen. They were looking for summer work. He was gone all day during the haying season, and there wasn't much for her to do. She struck up a kind of friendship with me. We talked over the fence a couple of times until he came home early one afternoon and ran me off with a shotgun. He probably wanted to beat me to a bloody pulp, but he knew he'd be run out of town. So he beat her instead.

"He was a lot older than she was, and jealous. I understand him better now, but when I was sixteen, I hated him. So when she asked me to help her run away, I was all for it. We worked it out that she'd wait until he passed out after one of his late-night drunks at the Wicked Eye. Then she'd come up to our place, and I'd drive her to the bus depot in Big Elk.''

Strider suddenly shoved his cold nose into my hand, and I jumped.

"The night she came, it was so late, I'd fallen asleep. The banging on the door and the screaming woke up the whole family. I didn't know it, but my mother had been locking the door at night. She didn't trust Gene. Your grandparents and your uncle Joe and I were all heading for the door when the blast came.''

Dad ran his fingers through his hair, rubbing his scalp the way he does when he has a headache. His voice slowed. "The pounding and the crying stopped when the shotgun went off. I remember staring at the door and hearing something soft and heavy sliding down it on the other side.

"I just stood there, watching her blood creeping toward me under the door. Then I started screaming— screaming at Gene for doing that to her and at the rest of us for letting her down.''

We stared at each other for a long time without saying anything. Finally I couldn't stand it any longer. "You really couldn't see her today?"

"No.''

"Then how come I can?"

"I don't know. Unless . . . unless it's because she thinks you're me.''

"Dad. . . .'' I didn't want this. My own personal ghost? Forget it. "How do I make her go away?"

Dad didn't answer right away. When he finally looked up at me, he looked old and tired. "Zach," he said quietly, "I've been asking myself that for twenty-five years.''

He half turned in his chair. I looked where he was

looking, at the oddly shaped stain like a watermark on the floor under the back door. Once a year Dad would do a spring cleaning and really give the floor a going over. When he was through, the shape would be different. I remember when I was seven, it looked like a brontosaurus. Now it looked like South America.

I'd never asked where it came from. I'd always figured it was just from water leaking under the door in the winter. Now I was staring at it and thinking about blood pumping out of a torn-up body slumped against the back door. "You mean . . . ?"

"Every year. I come in one morning during the first haying, and there's a new bloodstain on the floor under the door. I've tried sitting up all night more times than I can count, but I've never seen her . . . or heard her."

I wished Dad hadn't told me all this. It wasn't the Mennart place that was haunted. It was ours.

"Zach?"

"Yeah?"

"Something's different this year. Something has changed. If you can see her, maybe we have a chance to play the whole thing over again, make it come out differently."

"Dad . . . no way!"

"I've lived with this thing for too long, Zach. I don't want it hanging over you and your kids too."

I thought about sitting at this table twenty-five years from now with my son and telling him about the stain, passing on the burden. It was a bad thought. Dad was right. But how could we change something that had happened years ago?

In the next couple of days Dad and I talked about ways we might do it. He surprised me. He'd really read up on ghosts and the supernatural. Every time he went into Big

Elk, he'd spend a couple of hours at the public library. "Real nice librarian there," he said with a grin I was glad to see. Neither of us had been doing much grinning since this all started.

Dad figured that what brought Gene and Sue Ellen back year after year was unfinished business. When Sue Ellen died, she was beside herself with terror and desperation. Gene had been killed minutes later, out of his head with jealousy and rage. Their hearts had stopped beating between one breath and the next, but emotions that powerful and out of control needed some kind of resolution before they could die too.

What we were going to try to do was give them a chance to replay that moment and finish it one way or another. Get past it and leave it behind. Maybe then the passion and the fury could die too. That was Dad's theory anyway. He didn't know whether it was going to work or not, but he figured we had to try. I figured anything was worth trying if it would make them leave us alone.

Dad and I agreed that Sue Ellen should go on thinking I was him, so once she started talking to me, I let her call me Graham. She was real easy to talk to. Before I knew it, I was telling her about my dream of making the major leagues and about the great ideas Dad kept coming up with for helping me develop my pitching arm. Whenever I ran out of things to tell her, I'd try to find out more about her, but somehow she'd always manage to turn things around so we'd be talking about me again. She acted like I was the most interesting guy she'd ever known.

Every night at supper I'd tell Dad what we'd talked about. He was curious about whether we were replaying everything exactly the same way or whether there were differences. It wasn't exactly the same because I'm not Dad, but it seemed close enough.

One difference had begun to worry me, though. Dad said he'd only talked to Sue Ellen a couple of times over the fence before Gene broke it up, but a week went by without anything like that happening. Then Gene came home and scared the daylights out of me, just like he'd scared Dad.

I said "came home," but it was more like he materialized suddenly, roaring into the yard in his gray pickup. He was out of the cab, swearing at me, while the truck was still rolling to a stop.

He's not real, I told myself. *It's not a real gun.* But when the shotgun went off, the twigs and leaves that rained down on me from the oak tree over my head were real all right. Which meant that the pellets in his gun were real lead. I took off for home without looking back.

Sue Ellen was real too. I didn't have any trouble believing that. The first time my hand brushed hers, I jerked it away. I don't know what I was expecting, but her skin was as warm and solid as mine. And she didn't have any problems touching me—leaning against me when we sat on her back steps, holding hands when we were walking, rumpling my hair. I got used to being close to her pretty fast.

She had a husky laugh that made me feel like a high-wire artist—half-scared and half-exhilarated—and her perfume smelled like spring jasmine. After I'd had to untangle a confused bee from her long ponytail, I teased her about it, but I liked her smell. I liked everything about her, except her husband.

I began making up stuff to tell Dad. The things we were talking about were getting too personal and private. It made me wonder whether he'd felt the same way about her that I did, but I couldn't ask him without admitting I'd been lying about our conversations. So I kept everything—the wondering and my feelings about Sue Ellen—to myself. It was the first time I'd ever done something I didn't want Dad to know about, and I hoped he'd never find out. I'd have hated it if he thought he couldn't trust me anymore.

After the shotgun incident I didn't see her for a couple of days. Then one afternoon she was back at the fence— both eyes blackened, cuts healing on her swollen lip. When she tried to smile, the cuts made her mouth twist, and she winced. That's when I knew I was going to help her get away from Gene if I had to kill him myself.

We made the same plan she and Dad had made. She would come to our house late one night, and I'd drive her to Big Elk. Once we'd done all the planning we could, I stayed away from her. It was hard to do, but I wanted Gene to think he'd scared me off.

Dad and I still had some major questions about our own plan. What would happen if we *were* able to change the way things turned out? Where would Sue Ellen go once she was safely inside our house? And if Gene couldn't shoot her and then get shot himself, what would he do? What *could* he do? Would his jealousy and rage get even stronger, or would they dissipate once Sue Ellen was gone?

"I don't know, Zach," Dad kept saying. "I don't know. We just have to risk it."

Risk what? I kept wondering. I couldn't forget about the twigs and leaves raining down on me after the pellets from Gene's gun had passed through the oak tree. Maybe if I had known what we were risking I wouldn't have felt so cold and queasy . . . or maybe I would have felt worse.

Another thing we couldn't be sure about was when she'd be able to sneak away from Gene. To make sure we didn't miss her, I started camping out in the hayloft on the second floor of the barn at night, wrapping myself in the nose-tickling smell of new-mown hay as if its ordinariness could protect me from whatever out-of-the-ordinary things were coming.

On the third night, when the moon had sunk low enough to send out long shadows—each one shaped like a hiding man—I was hunched on the baled hay listening to an owl hooting on the other side of the meadow and wishing that I were somewhere else . . . or someone else maybe. Anything to get out of this—

A shrill cry, cut off abruptly, made me break into a sweat. The owl had found its prey. I checked out the pile of rocks I'd collected in case I needed ammunition, stretched and yawned, blocking out sound for a couple of seconds. When I closed my mouth again, I heard something else . . . the crunch of footsteps on gravel. Someone was running down our drive.

Then I heard a panting sound, *huh . . . huh . . . huh,* with a high, thin edge to it—half whimper, half sob. And finally I saw her—mouth open, hair flying, small, terrified squeaks bursting out of her with every step.

At first I couldn't see what was scaring her so much. There was no one on the road behind her. And then I saw the dark, massive shape racing through our pasture, aiming to cut her off. Moonlight glinted on the barrel of the gun as it swung up and back in his hand. "I'm warning you, Sue Ellen!" he roared. "Come back here, you bitch!"

She ran for the house, moaning in terror. Beside me Strider got slowly to his feet, hackles rising across his shoulders like the hair on the back of my neck.

Tripping on the porch step, she crashed against the kitchen door. I waited, expecting the door to open. With all the noise she was making, how could Dad not know she was there?

Gene was at the pasture gate, yanking furiously at the chain. I could see him clearly now. In a few more steps he'd be in the yard. She was banging on the door, crying, "Graham, Graham . . . !"

Strider began barking wildly, and suddenly I remembered why I was out here. To be Dad's eyes and ears. "Dad!" I screamed. "She's here! Open the door!"

The gate swung open, and the huge shape of the man froze for a second, head turning as he searched for me. But when the gun came up, it was aimed at Sue Ellen.

"Dad!" I screamed again, and hurled a rock at the man by the gate.

It hit. I heard him swear. And then the back door flew open. Light poured out across the yard. She half fell inside, and the door slammed shut. Gene was racing toward the house, his gun still raised.

"Lock it, Dad!" I screamed. "He's coming! Lock it!"

I was hurling rocks like crazy. Most of them were finding their mark, and they were hitting solid flesh, but they didn't stop him. He ran up to the door and tried the knob, jerking and shaking it and beating on the door with his fist. Then he stepped back, and before I could yell a warning, he fired a blast right through the wooden door.

"You creep!" I screamed. "If you've hurt my dad . . . !"

Whirling suddenly, Gene came off the porch and hit the ground running, heading in my direction. He ran through the barn door below me, screaming threats and curses at Dad.

The ladder to the loft began to bounce and shake. He was coming up fast. Coming after me! I had only one way to go. Out the loft door. It was a drop of ten or twelve feet, but I flung Strider out ahead of me and rolled on my stomach, ready to slide over the edge and drop.

I saw the gun first and then his head. He stared at me, his face so twisted with rage and hate that he looked like a madman from my worst nightmares. He wanted Graham dead. Telling him I wasn't my dad wasn't going to stop him now. As he came up the last few rungs of the ladder into the loft, I let go and dropped.

I'd done this jump before, but this time I was in too much of a hurry, landing on one knee and rolling over in the dirt. Scrambling up, I headed for the house. The distance between the barn and the house was only a hundred feet, but I was limping badly, and it seemed like a thousand yards. I didn't look back. I didn't have to. I knew where he was. Standing in the loft door aiming his shotgun at my back.

I made it to the back porch and fell. "Dad! Dad!" I was crying now, lurching forward on hands and knees. "Open the door! Quick, Dad. He's after me!"

I scrabbled desperately at the door, trying to reach the knob. *Dad . . . please hurry!*

Behind me a gun went off. I screamed. The door jerked inward, and I was dragged inside as a wave of heat swept over me. Sinking into a universe of darkness shot through with points of blood-red light, I thought, *I'm dying. I've traded places with Sue Ellen. . . .*

It has been two years since that night . . . two quiet years with no new stain. Graham keeps telling me to forget it, but I can't.

I was sick for a long time. The doctor couldn't figure

out what was wrong. Just a high fever and a lot of deliri-
ous nightmares. And he couldn't explain the holes in my
back—a pattern like buckshot, but no sign of lead in the
wounds. My father just said he didn't know what it was
either. How can you explain to someone that your son
was shot by a man who's been dead for twenty-five years?

Graham says that when he heard me yell the first time,
he flung open the door and a strong gust of wind blew
past him, bringing with it a faint smell of jasmine. Locking the door, he raced through the house, but if she was
still there, he couldn't find her. When he heard me banging on the door, he came tearing back into the kitchen
and was fumbling with the lock when he heard the shotgun blast.

It scared him so badly, he felt for a second as if pellets
were ripping into *his* gut. When he dragged me inside, he
was crying, and praying, and cursing Gene all at the same
time. But if Gene was still there, Graham never saw him
either.

Maybe I could forget about it if I didn't have to see my
father every day. He has a permanent streak of white in
his hair. He wears it like it is a badge of honor, but I wish
he'd dye it. Every time I look at him, it reminds me of
how much my life has changed since that night, and how
easily he got off when the whole thing was his fault from
the beginning.

He won't admit it—he says it's over and he doesn't
want to think about it anymore—but he and Sue Ellen
did more than talk over the fence. They must have. I
know how I felt about her, and Graham would have
reached the point of doing something about it a lot faster
than I did.

But all he has to show for the trouble he made for the
rest of us is a streak of white hair that his girlfriends think

is sexy. Gene and Sue Ellen are dead, and I'll have holes in my back for the rest of my life. Not just scars but holes. Girls think they're gross. Every time I take off my shirt, I have to try to explain them. It's easier to keep my shirt on.

I'll never play pro baseball either. By the time I could tell them how much my knee was hurting, it was too late to repair the damage.

Now I know why Mom left. She couldn't trust Graham anymore. When I graduate from high school this year, I'm moving out too. I know this place has been in our family for five generations, but my father can have it. I don't want it. Or him. I can make it on my own.

Was it worth the risk we took? Once a year I figure it was. The rest of the time I wish I'd never seen her. One thing I know for sure—you want to be careful about messing around with things that have already happened. Because when the past changes, the present and the future change too.

FRANCES A. MILLER

When she wrote her first novel for young adults, *The Truth Trap,* Frances Miller never intended that there be a sequel to it. But she started wondering what would become of Matt McKendrick, the main character who was accused of murdering his little sister. So she wrote *Aren't You the One Who . . . ?* and followed that with *Losers and Winners,* a story about Matt's rivalry with a black athlete as they compete for Runner of the Year. Miller recently ended the series with *Cutting Loose,* the story of Matt's return to the hometown he had run away from and a summer of challenges and changes spent working on a guest ranch with five friends before he heads for college. The American Library Association named the first book in that series a Best Book for Young Adults in 1980, and it later received the California Young Reader Medal.

Frances Miller has four grown children and lives in California with her husband, whose business took them to Australia for six years starting in 1977. That led to her organizing a nationwide gift of over five hundred American children's books and birthday cards to Australia's children in celebration of their Bicentennial in 1988.

Having been a "Book Fair Lady" as well as a reading and English teacher, Miller is currently a reference librarian. She is working on a new young adult novel as well as a fantasy for the middle grades and a picture book for younger readers.

It's been impossible for Troy to get Lida to notice him. Then one morning he gets lucky. . . .

TEETH

PATRICIA WINDSOR

The tooth was lying on the sidewalk, camouflaged against the erratic pattern of embedded oyster shells. But Troy had caught its alien shape. Curious, he bent down to pick it up.

It seemed real enough. A big molar with long roots, the enamel clean and white. Gingerly he sniffed at it, expecting a synthetic smell to signal that it was a fake, but braced for the reek of decay. There was no odor at all. He shrugged and put it into his pocket, wondering idly if finding a tooth meant good luck, like finding a penny.

When he got to school, Lida was standing right there on the steps. Troy's heart began its beat-skipping tricks, and as usual he tensed up, torn between fierce hope for a kind word or glance and resignation to the fact she didn't know he was alive.

"Hi, Troy," she said.

He walked right on past, head down as if waiting for a blow; it took that long for her words to sink in. When they did, he twisted around and almost fell.

"Hi . . ." he said uncertainly. "How're you doing, Lida?" It was amazing that he could speak.

"I'm doing just fine," she replied, brown eyes twinkling. "How 'bout you?"

"Fine," he mumbled, and trudged away. She was only playing with him.

At lunchtime in the cafeteria, as he was gazing down at the selection of wilted salads and curled cheese sandwiches, his best friend, Willie, came up behind him and put her arm around his shoulder. "Hey, Troy, what's this I hear about Lida being mad at you?"

Troy, reaching for a salad, paused in disbelief. "She's *mad* at me?"

Willie nodded, a crooked smile on her face. "She's telling everybody how you snubbed her this morning." Willie peered at him. "You feeling all right, Troy? I mean, you *snubbed* Lida? After all this time trying to get her to notice you?"

Troy was about to explain to Willie that it was a mistake; he hadn't meant to rebuff Lida, he'd just been too shy and uncertain to respond. Then an unfamiliar but favorable feeling of power swept through him. If Lida was angry with him, he had some kind of upper hand. "Yeah," he told Willie, swinging his tray off the rails. "Who does she think she is, anyway?"

Willie followed him to a table. "Way to go, Troy," she said, laughing. "Playing hard to get, right?"

Troy laughed with her. "Maybe." He felt so good. He didn't even bother to look around the room to find Lida in the crowd of students. Let her suffer.

But by evening the feeling of triumph had worn off. He hadn't heard anything more from Lida. He was right back where he started. Willie might have been wrong. Lida didn't care spit about him. He wished he knew what to do next. He phoned Willie for advice.

"Call her up or something," Willie said.

Troy felt a nervous chill. "You mean on the phone?"

"That's how it's usually done."

"I couldn't . . ."

"It's real simple, Troy. Just like you're talking to me right now."

"That's different. Talking to you is like . . ."

Willie sighed. "Yeah, I know, like talking to yourself."

Something in Willie's voice made him pause. "What's wrong? Now are you mad at me too?"

"Of course not. Call Lida, Troy. Get it over with."

He would, in a minute. When he got in the right mood. He drank a can of soda. He put a tape on. He flipped through his notebook and pretended to do some homework. The hands on the clock kept moving. Soon it would be too late to phone.

All at once he just did it. No need to look up her number; he'd had it memorized for months. Punched in the digits quickly, before he could change his mind. Two rings and she picked it up herself.

"Hi, Lida?"

"Who is this?"

"Me, Troy."

"You've got to be kidding." She made a derisive sound, half laugh, half snort, and hung up on him.

The next morning he kept rubbing his jaw. His mother wanted to know what was the matter.

"Nothing, just feels sore."

"Grinding your teeth in your sleep again, I bet."

He remembered the tooth. Got it out of his pocket and tossed it onto his bureau with the other junk. So much for good luck.

That afternoon he found another one. Coming back from the playing field, he saw it lying on the ground. Might have easily missed it. The shape caught his eye, looking incongruous there on the grass. He picked the tooth up, wondering how it could be here instead of home in his room. Then realized he was an idiot—it wasn't the same tooth. This one was slightly less dazzling. A little yellow around the edges, maybe the beginning of a cavity on the side. *Okay,* he thought, *let's see if this one brings better luck.* Of course he wasn't serious.

Lida was standing in the hall when he came out of the locker room. "Hey, Troy," she said. Her voice was softer than he had ever heard it. Vulnerable—was that the word?

"I'm sorry I hung up on you," she said, brown eyes melting into his. "It's just . . . I was hurt, you know?"

"Hurt?"

She lowered her lashes. His legs were turning into syrup. Gosh, she was beautiful.

"I thought you didn't like me anymore," she said.

"Like you? Lida, I . . ." He swallowed. He wanted to believe what was happening, that this was no cruel joke. "I could never be mad at you, Lida."

Her face lit up. She glanced around, then pecked a quick kiss on his face, missing his cheek, her lips glancing off his chin. "Troy, I'm so glad!"

He watched her walk away. His fingers caressed the spot she'd kissed. Had it really happened?

In math class he felt the soreness in his jaw again. He rubbed at it. Funny. As if Lida's lips had left the pain. He liked that. He could suffer through any pain she wanted to inflict on him. He was used to it.

His mother made him go to the dentist.

"Looks like a wisdom tooth coming in," the dentist said. "Nothing to worry about. You'll feel like a li'l ole baby for a few days." The dentist chuckled heartily. "But think of all those smarts that are coming in!"

Troy swabbed the sore gum with Anbesol and forgot the pain. It was nothing compared with how Lida was making him feel. She hadn't talked to him since yesterday. Acted as if nothing had happened between them. Troy was confused. Did she like him or not?

"She's trifling with me," he told Willie as they walked home together. It was hot for April. The newly bloomed azaleas hung their heads; the sun pushed through the shading of Spanish moss on the live oak trees; the air was hazy. Willie's upper lip was beaded with perspiration.

She shook her head. "It's the way the game is played, Troy. Romance is like that." Her voice was plaintive, somehow sad.

"Like a cat worrying a mouse," Troy said. "If this is romance, it's no fun."

But he felt mildly encouraged. He trusted Willie. If this was the way it was done, all right, he could take it. But he was afraid to phone Lida again in case she hung up. He locked himself in his room and lay on the bed. He'd been doing that a lot these last few days, neglecting his homework and chores. He put his finger into his mouth. The wisdom tooth had come in fast. Now another one was cutting through on the other side. What a joke, teething at his age.

Teeth. The second molar he'd found was there on top of his dresser with the first one. A crazy idea titillated his mind. What if he found another tooth? Would it make Lida talk to him again?

Troy searched the streets the next morning on his way to school, half serious, half as a joke. As if teeth would be lying around all over the place. He didn't find any.

"Visualization," Willie said at lunch, licking spaghetti sauce off her chin. "That's the way to get what you want."

Troy had been telling her his problem. On again, off again Lida. "How do you mean?"

"Make a picture of what you want in your mind. Visualize Lida saying she loves you."

"If she just agrees to go out with me, it's enough. Will it really work?"

Willie shrugged. "Some people believe it. My sister, for one. She's busy visualizing an engagement ring. Don't look so darn serious, Troy!"

She giggled, and Troy knew she was humoring him. Still, secretly he thought it was worth a try. He would visualize finding another tooth. It was weird, probably dumb, but he had to believe the teeth brought him luck with Lida. Well, maybe it wasn't so weird. It was like a rabbit's foot. He shut his eyes, saw himself walking home from school, saw the oyster-shell sidewalk glistening in the afternoon sun, saw the tooth lying there, saw himself bending down to pick it up.

"Earth to Troy, you still with us?" Willie was asking.

"Huh? Sure, just thinking," Troy said sheepishly.

"You were a thousand miles away."

The third tooth he found had a bad odor, like stale breath. It was dingier, too, and had a definite brown hole where a cavity had been, where maybe a filling had fallen out. Troy put it in his pocket. He felt a shiver go through him. A goblin pain of anticipation gripped his stomach.

That evening Lida phoned. She was nicer than she had ever been. Encouraged, he asked her out. She didn't exactly say yes, but then she didn't refuse either.

By morning another wisdom tooth had appeared in his mouth. Funny how they grew so fast.

When Troy found a fourth molar—this one had a hole where a filling had fallen out—his final wisdom tooth cut through. Probably coincidence, but Lida was suddenly warmer, more affectionate. The trouble was, it didn't last. One minute she was squeezing his hand, the next minute she was cold as ice. So he had to look for another tooth, crazy as it seemed. Anything to make her smile at him again.

After he found the fifth molar—stained, smellier, more decayed—Troy noticed something in the roof of his mouth. A strange sort of bump. A few days later a tooth pushed through. He looked at it in the bathroom, craning his neck awkwardly as he held his mother's makeup mirror. He was scared at the bizarre sight of it; teeth didn't belong in the roof of your mouth! He said nothing to his mother, not wanting another visit to the dentist. He felt somehow ashamed.

But this time Lida's attitude really changed. The attention she paid to him was not so short-lived. She actually walked part of the way home with him. Troy was aware that Willie straggled behind. He wished she wasn't there.

He began avoiding Willie. She had become an inconvenience; he was too busy with Lida. When Willie phoned, he told his mother to say he was out. Anyway, it hurt to talk on the phone so much. Especially at night, the extra teeth hurt. Sometimes he woke up just before morning, bathed in sweat, thinking he really should do something about it. Go to the dentist and have them all pulled out. But then he'd find another tooth on the street and Lida would be waiting for him on the school steps, smiling that special smile, eyes only for him, and he was afraid to do anything that might break the spell.

He was looking for teeth all the time now. "I've got to stop this," he told himself, and then went out and searched the sidewalks anyway. The collection of molars was growing. He hid them in his closet at first, but the smell was so bad, he had to take them outside and put them in the back of the tool shed.

By June nine new teeth crowded the roof of his mouth, and a tenth was breaking through under his tongue. It was really hard to talk now. He mumbled about dental surgery when the kids at school or the teachers gave him funny looks. It was a strain to keep his lips tightly closed around his overfilled mouth. Willie commented on his new reticence. That is, she spoke to him when she managed to catch up with him, or grab him unawares. He took different routes home; he sneaked through the lanes and other people's gardens to keep out of her way. But sometimes, in those early-morning panics, it was Willie he thought of. He loved Lida, but it was Willie who came to mind when he felt most scared.

Willie stopped him in the corridor one day, her grasp on his arm determined, almost fierce. "You don't talk to me anymore, Troy," she said, and worry creased her brow. He was tempted to reply, to tell her everything. But he couldn't find the words. Even if he could figure out what to say, he wouldn't be able to say it. That strange, shameful feeling welled inside him. And then there was Lida, coming down the hall, calling to him. Willie's face closed up.

"True love," she said, giving Lida a slit-eyed glance. "Smile, Troy, don't work so hard at it."

Smiles were a thing of the past. It was hard to smile without opening your mouth. His mouth felt like it was full of rocks. It was getting harder to eat.

"He has no appetite," his mother said. "I'm worried."

"He's probably in love," said his father, winking at Troy over the tops of his reading glasses. "Nothing to fret about. Just look at those chubby cheeks."

Troy studied himself in the bathroom mirror. He

looked like a squirrel with a face full of nuts. It wasn't funny. He fought an overwhelming desire to spit and keep on spitting, as if he could get rid of the teeth, which were like coarse, salty pebbles against his tongue. Only belief in Lida could drive the fearful sickness away. And yet hadn't she grown colder toward him again? Had that been Lida walking off after school with someone else?

The tooth he found the next day was the worst so far: greenish with mold, carious, its roots eaten away. The smell lingered in the air and on Troy's fingers. But in spite of its foulness, Troy caressed it. He didn't hide it in the shed but kept it in his pocket, so that he could touch it and know its power. He sensed that the rewards would be greater this time around. Lida would be his.

A plan unfolded; he knew just what to do. Ask her to go for an evening walk along the river, when the sun was fire falling behind the new bridge, when a cool breeze was picking up. There in the nearly dark he would have the courage he could never muster in broad daylight. In the shadows he could find the right words to speak. He trembled at the thought of holding her, kissing her lips.

He phoned her with confidence, knowing she would not refuse. She agreed readily to meet him on River Street. He showered and dressed carefully. He rinsed his mouth with Listerine, for once oblivious of the claustrophobic feeling of his teeth. He ran through the streets. No need to search the ground now.

She was waiting for him on the promenade. She seemed impatient, but her smile was unsullied, immaculate. He took her hand, and they began walking into the west, toward the bridge. He felt so happy. He felt as if his heart would burst.

Lida's voice, tinged with the slightest irritation, broke

the rapturous silence. "Cat got your tongue or something?"

He nervously fingered the putrid tooth in his pocket. He wanted to speak, to tell her how much he cared. But he was nervous about how the words would sound coming from the rabble of his mouth.

He wanted so much to kiss her. Better to kiss her and forget the words.

She stopped and leaned against the railing, looking out into the river. Faint sounds of music came from the restaurants behind them. The water was roiled by the paddle of the *River Belle,* getting ready to take the tourists over to the island.

"Sometimes you can see a dolphin here," she said.

He put his hand gently on her shoulder. Felt her tremble under his hesitant touch. She turned to him expectantly. The setting sun blazed in her hair. He had never seen her so beautiful.

He wished he could tell her: *Lida, I love you.*

She raised herself on tiptoe, so that her lips reached his.

Happiness burst in his heart. He put his own lips against hers and felt her responding, melting against him. He lost himself to her.

And then suddenly the heat of her body against his chest was gone. His lips felt the cold chill of night air. He opened his eyes.

She was backing away.

"My God," she said. "Oh, my God. Your mouth is full of teeth!"

Her rosebud lips were twisted in horror.

At that moment, before Lida's screams drew the attention of the passersby, before the people started staring and pointing at him, he wanted to shout that he was sorry. He wanted to go back in time. He wanted . . .

"Willie," he tried to say. But from his mouth came only the growling moan of suffocating decay.

PATRICIA WINDSOR

Known for her young adult mystery novels, such as *Killing Time, Diving for Roses,* and *Something's Waiting for You, Baker D.,* Patricia Windsor has recently added supernatural and horror elements to her books and short stories. In *The Hero,* for example, the main character is blessed/cursed with precognition, the ability to foresee accidents and tragedies. She combines the supernatural and horror with the stark reality of a serial killer who threatens girls in a small New England town in her most recent novel, *The Christmas Killer.* Her first novel, *The Summer Before,* was named a Best Book for Young Adults by the American Library Association, and *The Sandman's Eyes* won an Edgar Allan Poe Award from the Mystery Writers of America in 1986. Her short stories have appeared in *Seventeen* and other magazines all over the world.

She was born and raised in New York City but says she has become a vagabond who has lived in Boston, Chicago, Washington, and London, and resides in Savannah, Georgia—for now at least. In addition to writing, Patricia Windsor works as a crisis counselor and has taught creative writing at the University of Maryland and the University of South Florida as well as for the Institute of Children's Literature.

The carousel became Valerie's favorite attraction at the traveling carnival. But it wasn't just the ride that attracted her back to it night after night. . . .

THE HOPPINS

ANNETTE CURTIS KLAUSE

The carousel stood in the dark on a newly birthed midway. Quiet rang in the air like a silent bell—crisp, clear. Almost, the carousel animals breathed.

Then a shadow moved inside, and the shades of gray were punctuated by a fleck of red light that burst sporadically. A drift of smoke curled from between spiraled slim columns.

Hooves, muffled in fresh dust, gently thudded near, and a horse pulled an ancient caravan to a halt in front of the carousel. The scene froze for a moment in the timeless night, then the back door squeaked, releasing time; steps were lowered, and a young man emerged. He was carrying something that filled his powerful arms, something that suddenly twisted independent of his grasp. It was an elderly woman with useless legs. The same dark beauty marked their faces, his new, hers crumbled.

The figure in the glazed control turret flicked his cigarette away. A circle of white lights flared around the canopy and revealed him to be a small, middle-aged man in a raincoat and cap. He pulled his coat closer around him and shivered. He made no effort to step out and meet the couple approaching him.

The young man climbed the steps of the carousel and began weaving a circuit between the animals. The lights picked out the gold of the charm he wore around his neck, setting the five-pointed star of the pentagram afire against his smooth, dark skin. His companion was cob-web-light, yet he moved slowly, as if through water. The woman began a low, tuneless humming that gradually formed itself into words with syllables that sometimes spat and sometimes hissed. She tossed a fine powder into the air from a pouch in her lap. The carousel, viewed through the mist of it, writhed.

Three times around they circled, then they stopped by a slinking wooden wolf. The woman ceased her chant, grunted, and shook out the final contents of the bag. The young man looked down at her, and she nodded.

"It's renewed," she said.

Shifting her in his arms, he took a package from her and flung it to the carousel's middle. "It's going to take more than that this time, else he'll be too desperate to hold," he said to the woman. The control-room door opened a crack, and he grinned a feral leer, all flash of teeth. "Do your job," he called out. He carried the woman back down the steps and to the caravan.

"What luck I have with husbands, boy," the sarcastic old voice croaked as he closed the caravan door. "The first one loped and the second one cringes."

They drove off, leaving the older man to creep out of his refuge and find at its door a clot of raw flesh wrapped in aromatic leaves.

It was the night before the Hoppins.

Once a year the Hoppins came. All the traveling carni-vals in the north of England, small and large, made their pilgrimage to the town moor at Newcastle-upon-Tyne in a journey that seemed to the locals as much an inevitable part of nature as the migration of swallows. But to Valerie it was still new. All week the caravans, trailers, and lorries materialized as if conjured by the same magic that awoke the early blooming of summer dresses. On her trips into town on the bus Valerie was tantalized by glimpses of mysterious architecture rising where previously only cows had grazed. She waited breathlessly for opening night, when a new landscape would exist—a garish, shrieking, laughing, churning madness that would stretch for miles.

On the night before opening, she invaded her bank and counted out her money, separating it into equal piles —one for each day of the fair. Her sleep was restless, permeated with swirlings, swingings, and flights through color and light. A black dog chased her down a crowded midway, and she laughed but was frightened. She tripped over a tent peg and woke to her mother calling her for breakfast—"Rise and shine!"

Valerie couldn't get away until afternoon. Her mother seemed to take it as a personal insult that she wanted to go so urgently. "You don't have to be there when the gates open," she said, and found something else for Valerie to do. "At fourteen maybe you should be more interested in boys than in fairgrounds. But, then again, thinking of that Susan Millclough down the road . . ."

At last it was time to leave. "Don't be home late, just because it's the weekend," Mum called as Valerie left, and Valerie rolled her eyes heavenward.

The bus ride took forever. When it finally arrived at the town moor, she clattered excitedly down the metal stairs from the top deck and jumped off the platform. Even across the main road she could smell the wonderful smells, and they grew stronger as she ran up the path toward the first booths. The savor of onions and hot dogs, something she was never given to eat at home, sent out almost tangible fingers to escort her politely into the fair. The gentle warmth of the June air intensified as she reached the midway, so she slipped out of her light jacket and slung it over her shoulder. Digging her hand into her jeans' pocket, she found a barrette to hold back her pale hair.

The fair was packed already. Men laughed and argued over rifles at a stand. Screams shattered the air at intervals, as if gulls circled above. Barkers cozened her as she passed—"Step right up! Step right up and have a go!" The boys who worked on the stands had shaggy hair, shabby clothes, and cheeky faces. The women were often fat and wore cheap cotton prints, and white socks with their shoes.

The first ride she passed was the Caterpillar. It blasted her with hot, oily air from the diesel engine that drove it. The rumble of the engine obscured only briefly the raucous pop music pounding from the speakers so loudly that the sound was distorted. It took her seconds to identify the tune—not one she liked. She passed by. There would be other Caterpillars down the way. They weren't unusual. Anyway she just wanted to look for a while.

She finally succumbed to a Waltzer painted red and yellow, with laughing clown faces around its inner turret. It wasn't the most exotic ride but was always one of her favorites nonetheless. And after she had whirled and twirled, the ice was broken, and she started to spend.

She tried to win a goldfish with six Ping-Pong balls, but not one popped into the little fishbowls meant to receive them. *Oh, well,* she thought. *The stupid things are guaranteed to die three hours after you win them anyway.*

Valerie wished she had someone to share the fair with. Her family had moved to Newcastle over a year ago, just in time to discover last season's Hoppins, but she was a shy girl and, after a lonely summer, could never break into any of the close-knit groups at school. Those people had known each other for years, and there didn't seem room for someone new. At least she didn't get teased or jeered at like some misfits. In fact no one seemed to know she existed at all—especially boys.

She looked with curiosity at every young man she passed. *Do I fancy him?* she thought. *Would he like me?* This had become an enjoyable pastime lately. Her romantic fantasies were mostly inspired by the stories she read in the girls' magazines she bought each week with her saved lunch money and hid in her bedside table. But the next seduction that came her way was in the form of candyfloss—pink, sticky, and insubstantial. It seemed only right to have some her first day. Afterward she began to wish that she hadn't, because her hands felt unbearably sticky and there was no place to wash. She licked around her lips really well so she wouldn't end up with dirt clinging to her mouth like many of the children being dragged along by overheated parents.

The midway was already trampled down to dust and grass tufts. Straw from packing cases blew in the eddies of air from swirling rides and rumbling engines. Valerie tried the Spider, the Comet, and the Wall. She lingered by the sideshows, enjoying the lurid paintings. The outsides were the most interesting part; they always disappointed inside. *The Snake Woman—see her change in front of your very eyes!* She drops her cape to show her sequined suit. *Freaks! Freaks!* All bottled in formaldehyde, all dead. There were some sideshows she wasn't allowed into, you had to be eighteen. Valerie knew it had to be something to do with sex, but she'd love to know how much.

Between the stalls and the rides were the back streets

of the fair. From the midway she could catch glimpses of trailers, caravans, and washing hanging out to dry, growing smudgy with the fumes in the air. Machines like abandoned monsters waited to be fixed. The crowd streamed past her in either direction, all ages and all types: smart, middle-class couples with neat children; smiling old people heading for the Bingo; and street urchins staring, thumping each other, and haranguing the sideshow barkers.

Halfway down the fair Valerie saw the carousel. It was motionless, waiting for the next ride to begin. *Ah,* she thought. *A proper roundabout.* The only ones she'd seen so far were the little ones for "the kiddies," as the signs said. Their tiny trains and fire engines were much too small for her. This one looked old—a Victorian one perhaps. It had all the right kind of gingerbread decorations and prancing wooden horses that went up and down as well as around and around. She set off toward it. A carousel ride would be nice.

There were only a few passengers, but it must have been enough, because the music grew louder and the carousel began to move slowly. As she came closer, Valerie saw that the carousel held other animals besides horses. A giraffe went by and brought a smile to her lips. There was a lion, then a sea horse in the inner circle of animals, and then a unicorn near the edge. "Oh, lovely," she breathed softly to herself, admiring its gilded horn. Another group of horses came into view, stretching as if in full gallop, with flying wooden manes and flaring nostrils. Behind them came a big dog loping along.

No, it wasn't a dog, it was a wolf—a much too hungry-looking wolf for a fairground ride. Its muzzle was wrinkled back, revealing long fangs; its gums were painted a lurid red; and it had glittering glass eyes. It seemed to run purposefully behind the horses, ready to snap at their heels. No wonder they're running, she thought. She saw that someone had spilled the paint when coloring its lolling red tongue, and a few drops had splattered its chest. They looked like blood. "God, who'd want to ride on that thing?" she muttered to herself, and shuddered. She left, turned off the carousel now, and headed farther down the fair.

After the carousel, nothing attracted Valerie much and, on top of that, the diesel fumes were giving her a headache, so she headed for the bus stop. The tardy June dusk was still fading; at least she wouldn't be home late enough to annoy her mother.

Late Sunday afternoon Valerie left her quiet suburb again for the roar of the fairgrounds. "Don't worry. I'll get something for tea down there," she called to her parents, and ran out before they could object.

On the way down she studied the outfits the other girls on the bus wore. If only her parents would buy her decent clothes. Why couldn't they understand that you had to wear the right thing to be noticed? *I'm slender,* she thought. *I could wear lots of things well.* She got off the bus, pretending that she wasn't wearing an old T-shirt and jeans that weren't tight enough.

Valerie walked down the midway, looking for all the details she'd missed the day before. She bought a toffee apple, but spent much of the time getting the toffee out from between her teeth. She was sure they didn't used to be so troublesome. She wandered aimlessly. Not much interested her at this end now, maybe it was better farther down. She was looking for something, but she wasn't sure what. It was starting to make her feel a bit ill-tempered.

The hot, sweet, spindly scent of candyfloss crawled

through the air. It felt like strands of it were wrapping themselves around her esophagus in a stranglehold, and she had to keep clearing her throat. Finally she bought a Coke, but that also seemed too sweet and didn't quench her thirst.

She came upon the carousel again and couldn't help stopping to have a look. It was at a standstill while a young man, perhaps in his early twenties, collected fares from the customers waiting on their chosen mounts. His dark, thick hair crept over the collar of his open-necked denim shirt. He had a hairy chest. Last year she might have dismissed him as too grown-up because of that, but now it seemed sort of sexy. He wasn't exceptionally tall, but he looked powerful. She was fascinated by the way his rolled-up sleeves displayed his muscled arms. She suddenly noticed a fluttering feeling in her stomach and blushed. *Maybe opposites do attract,* she thought.

Valerie still felt slightly repelled by the carousel, yet she found herself hesitantly climbing the wooden steps to the platform. She mounted a horse as far away from the unsavory wolf as she could manage. The young man came for her money and scowled as he pocketed the coins. She blushed again. Did he know she'd been looking at him?

As soon as he left, the girls on the horses in front started to talk about him. "Eeeee! He's a canny lad, divvent ya think?" gushed one. The other, who was wearing gobs of makeup, blurted the typical Geordie catchall response, "Eeeee! Why aye."

From the way they talked and acted, Valerie recognized them as the type who lived in the council estate near the school. It wasn't that she was a snob exactly, she just felt a little nervous around them. It seemed to her that the girls at school from that neighborhood were a lot wilder than she could ever be, even if her parents gave her the chance. Valerie wasn't sure if she approved of them or not; they just made her feel uncomfortable. *They're talking loud enough for him to hear,* she thought, aghast. She lowered her eyes in embarrassment for them.

The music blared louder, signaling the start of the ride. Guitars clashed above her head, and a raucous voice screamed love lyrics in sadistic glee. If the old wood creaked, nobody heard. Her brow wrinkled, and she tapped irritably at the footrests. It didn't feel right. *There should be organ music or something. What was that old piping instrument they used in the old days? A calliope,* she thought.

The carousel picked up speed. "Blast!" she spat under her breath. She'd chosen a horse that didn't go up and down. The carousel moved faster and faster. The girls in front leaned across to each other, crowing gossip above the music. *Why do they even bother riding?* Valerie wondered. Groups of bystanders flashed into view and out, then reappeared again in quicker and quicker succession, caught in vignettes like cheap snapshots.

All too soon the music switched to a slower number, and the carousel changed its tempo to match. The ride was over. It seemed so short.

She decided to ride again. The girls in front left, so she moved up to one of their horses—an up-and-downer. The fare collector came around again. She fumbled, handing him her money, and one coin escaped, bounced from her thigh, and landed in a crack between the boards. He bent to pick it up while she stammered an apology. As he rose, he stopped briefly and tipped his head as if listening to something. It was only a moment, then he resumed moving. With a thickness in her throat she realized he was taking his time to inspect her. As he straightened up, his gaze lingered on her breasts. She turned her head away quickly, heart thumping, cheeks burning. How could he? She couldn't get comfortable on her perch and, squirming this way and that, discovered she was excited despite herself.

The ride started up again, and music boomed and clawed. The lights were brighter now that the sun was going down; as the carousel picked up speed, they left trails in the dusk. Her horse plunged up and down, and anonymous faces came and went at the perimeter. Surely it was faster this time, and the music louder. She could see people's mouths moving as she passed, but all she could hear was distorted rock and roll, as if she were trapped behind glass with the music. Her stomach lurched. *Not motion sickness now,* she thought. *I shouldn't have eaten that toffee apple on an empty stomach.*

She clutched her dipping mount with hands and knees and looked wildly at the control booth in the center. This *was* too fast. She could feel the wooden structure straining. Sticky candyfloss smells combined with diesel fumes to turn rancid in her lungs. The music tore at her ears; it suffocated her mind. She was sure the carousel would fly apart. But just before the bolts shook loose and threw her topsy-turvy into the gasping crowd, the ride began to slow and gradually settled to an uneasy halt.

Valerie dismounted the moment it was possible and, on unsteady legs, made her way down the steps.

As if to mock her, the young man called out in a deep voice, "Step up! Step up! Every third ride a fast one."

She was furious with him. It was all right for other rides, but it was obscene for a roundabout to go that fast. It was like abuse of an antique or something.

Valerie's taste for rides was gone for the evening. She decided to try her hand at Bingo instead. She lost. The only people she had ever known to win were her dad's parents, who had closets full of plaster wall plaques and cheap plastic appliances that they never used. She gave up and went into a freak show and tried to figure out how they attached the extra limbs to the few animals there. The most interesting thing was the fetus of Siamese twins in a jar. She wondered if that was fake also.

When it was late enough to go home, she walked up the midway toward the top-field exit. She was halfway there before she admitted to herself that she was only going that way because she wanted to pass the carousel again. *Stupid!* she chided herself. She tried to force herself to go by without looking, but she couldn't help it.

He was there, very close, lounging against the carved wolf, and looking right at her. When he saw she had seen him, he grinned slowly, raising his lips in a languid half snarl, half leer. His teeth were extremely white. His tongue was too red and seemed a little too large for his mouth. He reminded her of a dog that smelled heat, then she realized what that implied. She hurried past, unable to hide the anger on her face.

By the time the bus left Valerie at her stop, the large face of the moon was high, turning the night strangely bright. Ironically the shadows were all the darker because of the contrast, deep and concealing. Valerie skirted them carefully. The hedge in front of her house loomed like primeval forest. "I'm going to trim that bloody thing," Valerie promised herself as she hurried around it and onto the path. As she unlocked the front door and entered the warm, yellow hallway, she felt an unaccountable relief.

On Monday Valerie had to wait until after tea to go down to the fair. Some of the students went straight after school, but Valerie thought she would die if a good-looking boy saw her in her school uniform.

Valerie's mother wasn't thrilled with her going down to the fair on a school night. "But it's only once a year, after all, and you're a good girl," she said. Her dad hadn't come home from work yet, so Valerie didn't have to deal with him. She bolted down her salmon sandwiches and tea and left before her mother could change her mind.

"Don't be late, Val," Mum called from the door.

That night Valerie ignored the other rides and went straight to the carousel. She'd been thinking of the dark-haired man all day at school. She wasn't sure whether you called someone that age a man, but he certainly wasn't a boy—not like the ones at school anyway. She'd kept on visualizing him in her mind—the curl of his lips and his muscular arms especially. It made her intensely uncomfortable to think of his body, but she couldn't seem to stop. In math Mr. Thomas had told her to stop fidgeting, and she'd blushed bright red, for one paranoid moment afraid that her thoughts were broadcasting to all around her. But of course no one knew. She'd spent much time convincing herself that it was just the lighting the previous night that had made the man on the carousel look so peculiar. He was a bit rough, that was all. Anyhow she wouldn't talk to him. She just wanted another look.

It was a big letdown when she discovered he was nowhere to be seen in or around the carousel. There was another person, an older man wearing a dirty raincoat, running the ride. She tried to shrug off her disappointment and find other things to amuse herself with, but it was difficult after waiting all day.

She wandered around the game stalls, halfheartedly surveying the prizes wrapped in cellophane, the rows of cheap plaster cats and dogs, and the clumsily painted vases made in Hong Kong. The rubbish was already a plague along the midway, even though it was still early in the week. The old oil drums placed to collect the refuse were piled high. But still, the winking lights and bright displays were hard to resist for long, and she soon found herself seduced by the excitement again.

At one point, getting out of a bumper car, she thought she saw him in the crowd. She caught her breath in surprise. Jumping from the platform, she stumbled over a tent peg and almost collided with a grinning old woman. The woman grabbed Valerie's arm for balance; her grip was unexpectedly tight. Before Valerie finished her apology, she saw him again, turning to leave, and she knew she had to catch up with him.

She plunged into the milling crowd, brushing at the nettle rash tingling on her arm. She twisted frantically this way and that to get through the people crushing around the rides. A bulky woman with a screaming baby in her arms blocked her way, and she lost sight of him. Where had he gone? People seemed to deliberately get in front of her. She wanted to scream with frustration, kick people aside, elbow them out of her way. She caught another glimpse of him ahead. She pushed through a group of indignant teenagers and found herself between two cheaply constructed sideshows in time to see a leg disappear around back. She followed, darting around the corner eagerly—only no one was there, just three ancient caravans badly in need of paint, old gypsy caravans with carved scrollwork and faded lettering.

It suddenly struck her—what was she going to do when she caught up with him? The absurdity of her behavior became painfully clear. What on earth was she thinking of? *My God, I could have made a total fool out of myself,* she thought. *He doesn't even know me.* Her gut twisted with shame, and she was thankful no one could see her there.

It was very dark, she noticed. Not even moonlight

reached this spot. The only light came from a kerosene lantern over the door of the caravan to her left. It drenched the red and yellow steps like a theater spotlight, but just dimly reached the other caravans. There were no horses. She thought perhaps they were grazing farther out on the moor. Strangely, she couldn't hear the fair anymore. This made her uneasy. She was getting colder and colder and, without knowing it, had begun to hug herself. There was something wrong with her eyesight. No matter how hard she tried to focus, the caravans changed shape subtly in a distastefully organic way, bulging gradually in places, then subsiding like membranes that trapped sluggish things, better unseen. An oily nausea rolled up her gullet.

Now she could hear something, after all. Was it from a sideshow? No, it was coming from behind the middle caravan. Her skin felt as if a million tiny insects were crawling on her. She rubbed at her arm again.

Then she knew what it was she heard. It was growling— hollow, menacing growling—and it was growing louder, growing closer. She backed away, her heart threatening to explode. It was growing even louder, growing nearer still.

It burst upon her—a hurtling ball of fur, froth, blood, rolling, tumbling, slashing.

Her voice was trapped within her. She went flying and landed jarringly on red and yellow steps. She struggled to scream. The shape exploded apart into many legs and gleaming teeth.

"Two dogs!" she cried, dragging air down into rebellious lungs. "Two rotten dogs, that's all." They barreled into the darkness, still snapping and snarling.

Valerie pulled herself to her feet, shaking beyond control. She held on to the steps with her head down, breathing deeply, trying to get a grip on herself. Gradually she relaxed and straightened up. Raising her left hand to brush her hair back, she noticed her palm. Her grip on the carved step had left an impression there—a five-pointed star was stamped into the creased flesh like a brand. She had no idea why, but it frightened her more than anything had in her entire life.

"Yes," she heard a voice hiss.

She looked up at the caravan door in shock. There was a blood-red circle on it, and within that the black silhouette of a wolf's head. The eyes were slits that allowed the background red to blaze through. Someone started to laugh inside, throaty and low, and so quiet as almost not to exist. It sounded malicious and evil. Then, beginning as subtly as the laughter, the stink of rotten flesh drifted from beneath the door. She inhaled the fetid stench before she could help it, and gagged.

She turned and ran. She fled past lights, music, angry faces, shrieking hucksters, and tumbling trash cans, out into the cool, sweet night of the open moor.

She reached the bus stop just in time to catch the ten thirty-five bus home.

By Tuesday evening Valerie had managed to convince herself that she'd been really silly the night before. *I was just wound up,* she thought. *It's what I get for being by myself too much. I imagine stuff to make life exciting.* It would be dumb not to go to the fair because of an overactive imagination.

By seven o'clock she was in the line for the Ferris wheel. She was behind some girls from school. They giggled as they talked about rock stars and boys. Valerie wanted to say hello, but every time she tried, her mouth dried out and her hands started to tremble. Finally one girl looked her way, but when Valerie smiled, the girl looked right through her as if she didn't exist, then turned back to her friends' conversation.

Valerie felt miserable. Was she that invisible? Around and around on the Big Wheel she cursed her shyness, and the hollow in her belly was from more than the steep drop. *What does a person do?* she wondered. The magazines said to join clubs and participate in sports, but she couldn't think of anything she was good at. Anyhow, she was afraid. What if she went to one of those after-school clubs and they treated her like slime? That would be worse.

The ride was a waste. She'd been too busy agonizing to enjoy it. She left frustrated and annoyed.

It was with some perversity that Valerie decided to ride the Ghost Train. *You want spooky, you'll get spooky,* she told herself. She enjoyed it thoroughly: the numbing, jolting ride through the dark, the cobwebs on her face, the sudden appearances of luridly lit, badly formed waxworks lurching toward her, the hysterical screaming, and even the undertone of menacing laughter. She screamed as loudly as possible on all the right cues, in unison with the strangers in the carts up front and behind. It felt great. But at the end everyone descended with dignity from the rickety little carriages and walked away without looking at each other, in a minuet of secrecy.

Valerie wove in and out of the sights, smells, and sounds of the fair. The calls of barkers and hucksters filled the air: "Step right up! Step right up!" "Two fat ladies—eighty-eight!" "Make the children happy!" "Never before seen . . ." "Knock it down, take it home!"

Then, of course, she found herself in front of the carousel.

He was there, collecting fares, as surly as usual, keeping himself to his personal island of gloom and silence amid the noise of the fair. *What the heck,* she thought, and found an unoccupied horse. She wondered if he was really that great after all. He didn't seem like a particularly pleasant person, no matter if he was sexy-looking. She thought that perhaps the dark and moody type was all very well, but you certainly wouldn't have much fun with someone like that.

He reached her in his circuit about the ride, and as she handed him her coins, he stared at her face. Suddenly he smiled, taking her by surprise. "Back again then, luv? Glad you like the old girl." He pocketed her money, winked, and moved on.

Valerie was stunned. What had come over him? She knew she wasn't gorgeous, but he remembered her. *God, maybe he fancies me,* she thought, and almost giggled out loud in delight.

That ride was the best she'd ever been on. Her heart soared to meet the gay music that drove the engine of the carousel with magic. *He should smile more often,* she thought. What teeth. He could do toothpaste advertisements.

On the next ride he asked her name. She softly told him, not daring to raise her eyes. She couldn't think of anything else to say, and he moved on. She wished desperately that she were bright and witty, but it was as if he carried a force field around him that sent her body haywire whenever she passed through its radius and left her even more speechless than usual.

On the third ride he told her his name—Steve. That was vaguely disappointing. She thought, somehow, that his name would have been more unusual and romantic. He gently curled her fingers back around the money she held out to him. "On the house," he said. "If you want to stay and ride for a while."

It was only after he left that she realized with panic that if he didn't collect her fare, then he had no reason to come back. But she didn't have to fear, he came back. It was between rides mostly, sometimes just to laugh and wink as he passed, sometimes to stop and say a few words. Nothing he said was deep, but she treasured each utterance, reexamining it in minute detail so as not to miss any nuance. She felt special, but rather silly at the same time. *I'm an honored guest on a merry-go-round,* she thought with amusement.

By the time it was too late to stay a second longer, he had coaxed out of her where she went to school, how old she was, and the fact that she had a much younger sister —not exactly her life story.

"School night," she mumbled breathlessly when he raised his eyebrows as she dismounted.

He caught her hand, forcing her to look at him. "Come back tomorrow," he half asked, half demanded in a husky whisper. He traced a circle on her palm.

She smiled quickly, recapturing her hand, and escaped before she would have to say more.

He turned once from his round to watch her as she scurried through the crowd, one of his hands resting on the head of the stiff, cold wolf. His eyes caught the artificial lights above him and reflected them with the same crisp sparks as the glass eyes that glittered just below his fingertips.

Wednesday night, after an eternal day, Valerie arrived breathless at the fair. Ignoring the other entertainments, she headed straight for the carousel. She had agonized over what to wear. It was even more important now. She had finally settled on her same old jeans, but paired with a short-sleeved, low-cut cotton sweater she had hardly ever worn before because it emphasized her breasts to an almost embarrassing degree. She had left home quickly before she lost her nerve.

All sorts of fears chased through her mind. *What if he wasn't there? What if he was just playing with her last night? What if he didn't recognize her? Maybe he chose a different girl each night.*

But he was there; he did recognize her; and as soon as the carousel stopped, he beckoned her up. He helped her onto the unicorn. "This one goes up the highest," he explained. "And anyway it suits you." His hand rested on the small of her back, while his eyes appreciated her sweater. "Nice," he said, and grinned. She blushed, and he changed the subject. "The old man's here, so I've got to charge you, but he leaves at seven." She produced some change; he took it and left.

His hair had a newly washed gloss; it was thick and luxurious. His lips looked sensual and inviting, and she wondered what it would be like to kiss them. She'd never kissed anyone, so it was hard to imagine, but she was sure it would be wonderful. He seemed a little more forward tonight. Maybe she was giving him the wrong impression, but then, maybe she did want to encourage him—just a little.

She wondered where he was from. There was a tinge of some accent in his voice that she couldn't place. It was a thrilling voice, deep and resonant—at least it set off vibrations in her. *I bet he's really experienced,* she thought. She hardly dared imagine.

Between each ride he came for a visit; each time he touched her; each touch lingering longer, until he was caressing her neck or holding her hand. Her words came easier as she was slowly broken to his touch. Sometimes he rode beside her on the planks as the carousel moved, and she inhaled the warm muskiness of him until it made her out of breath. She wished those girls from school were watching her now.

Occasionally she would catch the older man looking at her, but she couldn't decipher the look on his face. Sadness perhaps? Why would he be sad?

Finally he called out, "Hey, Stephan! I gotta go. Time to stop flirting and take charge."

Ooo! Stephan sounds much more romantic, she thought. To cover her fluster, she asked quickly, "Why does he always wear a raincoat? I mean, it's not going to rain, is it?"

"Says he's always cold," Steve answered.

Steve was halfway to the control booth when Valerie noticed the old man was coming in her direction. Steve glanced back and must have remembered something. "Hey!" he called. It must have startled the old man, because he flinched.

Steve strode back and put an arm around the man's shoulders. "I forgot to tell you . . ." He led the man off the carousel. Valerie could see them talking. Steve smiled at the man, his teeth white and perfect. He gripped the man's shoulders and shook him playfully. Valerie could see the muscles of Steve's arms tense with controlled power, and a delicious snake uncoiled low inside her. Steve gave the old man a final pat on the back, and the man left. His hands were shaking. Valerie wondered if he drank.

Steve could no longer ride beside her, but from his station at the controls he sent her glances and winks that sustained the flirtation. When he collected fares, he was as abrupt as ever toward the other passengers; his smiles were just for her.

She had to leave the ride at times during the evening—whoever heard of getting saddlesore from a carousel horse? But she didn't stay away for long. She couldn't bear to.

One time she left in a panic when he brushed the side of her breast gently with his fingertips. But she talked herself back. *He didn't mean to, it was an accident,* she told herself. And part of her hoped he'd do it again.

The night streamed by, and it became later and later. There were fewer riders now. The crowd was thinning.

"I have to go now," she finally told him. "The last bus . . ."

"No. Stay here," he urged. "We'll be closing down soon. I've got a friend's car. I'll drive you."

She hesitated, while his fingers stroked the back of her neck hypnotically. She would be in terrible trouble, coming home that late. She gathered her willpower to say no and leave, but then he leaned forward and gently kissed her lips—warm and dry.

"All right," she whispered, averting her eyes and tugging nervously at the hem of her sweater. *Bother my parents,* she thought. *I'm always good.*

She was the only rider on the last ride. After that he came to her. "Listen, the old man will be coming back soon to close up and count the take. He shouldn't see you here this late. I don't want him getting the wrong idea about you."

"Does it matter?" she asked, getting off the unicorn. She was flattered by his protectiveness.

"Of course. Come back in half an hour. He'll be gone then. I'll leave some lights on."

"But I don't have a watch."

"Here, take mine."

She took the heavy, man's watch hesitantly and put it

in her pocket. Before she could go, he slipped his arms around her, and his sleepy-eyed look drew her into another kiss. This time her lips parted slightly in response.

She wandered the almost-empty fairgrounds, watching the carnival being put to sleep. Stalls were boarded up and locked, rides covered with canvas, engines shut down, and refreshment wagons rolled away. She wondered if she should just leave while she could. But it was too late to change her mind now—it was either drive with him or walk, and it was a long walk. Anyhow she had his watch; she had to give it back to him.

In the distance she heard the clang of rubbish bins being emptied. Darkness crept into the fair as bright lights blinked out, until only a few remained here and there, single stars left from constellations. She glanced at the watch frequently.

The night became chilly, and a small wind rose to chase a paper cup down the midway. Now and again someone called good night to a friend. After it had been a while since she'd seen anyone, she looked at the watch. It didn't seem possible, but there were still ten minutes to go. Hugging herself against the chill, Valerie wandered a bit farther, but the fair was a little scary now that it was dark, so she turned and made her way quickly back to the carousel. So what if she were a few minutes early?

Her stomach twisted into guilty knots. She was really going to get it when she arrived home. She could say that she had lost track of time, missed the last bus, and had to walk. How long would it take to walk that far? What if they asked why she hadn't phoned? Oh, gosh! *I don't want to think about it right now,* she decided. *Why can't I do something for myself for a change?*

Most of the carousel lights had been extinguished, only the outer circle of red bulbs remained lit, and liquid light pooled around the ride. The occasional flicker of a bulb caused the shadow animals to dance unnaturally.

Valerie climbed the wooden steps, and the hollow echo set off an answering chord of loneliness inside her. All was still. The control-booth windows reflected only black and points of red. She was afraid for a moment that no one was there, then she saw a shadow-clad figure near the center. She walked toward him, nervous about what to expect, yet eager to find out.

As she passed the giraffe, the temperature dropped. As she passed the lion, it grew colder still. *Unseasonable,* she vaguely thought.

He wound her in with unspoken promises and, the nearer she came, the more brittle the air, until it nearly snapped with ice. Her mind numbed and slowed with cold, but she still thought of warm embraces.

He stepped to meet her, his face etched in crimson and hollowed by night. His eyes emptied into another universe where reason still crept on all fours. He had discarded his shirt, and the thick, taut ropes and slabs of his body vibrated on the brink of a leap. His face was contorted, as if he felt a pain strangely pleasurable. His fingers twitched, as his hands reached for her, still with a hint of caresses. She slid into his embrace, and she heated with response despite the cold, her body slickening, still misinterpreting his desire.

"We are so glad you came back," he uttered harsh and low.

"We?" A tooth of cold pierced her ribs.

"My father and I," he breathed. "I'm afraid he's not allowed off the carousel these days. He causes too much trouble. But he enjoys visitors."

Her brows knotted in a quick question, but then she heard the creaking behind her. She broke from his arms and whirled around in time to see the wooden wolf pull and snap its right forepaw from its setting on the planks. Before she could move, she was grasped tightly from behind, and the man who held her immobile against him could contain his moans no longer.

The wolf laid its first paw on the deck, then, with more creakings and snappings, freed its other limbs from the prison that rarely let him go. Fear beyond her every belief stole her voice and left her gasping for a scream.

The painted hairs were rising from the wolf's neck, prickling like quills from the solid hackles. Its jaws gaped wider. Its tongue curled from between razor teeth. The red lights of the carousel reflected from its eyes and dyed its fur the color of blood.

The wolf took its first stiff step toward her, and the wood jerked and rippled into flesh. As the last rear paw shivered into being, the wolf began to growl, and a long, thin line of drool descended from its jowls. The moaning behind her crescendoed into choked snarls, and the arms around her tightened and roughened with fur. Nails sliced skin.

In the distance female laughter pealed, spiteful and knowing.

As the wolf crouched to leap, her head was yanked back by her hair, exposing her throat, and a hand crushed her breast. Frost iced the air with diamonds, and her mind shattered slowly, delicately, before the first savage wound.

ANNETTE CURTIS KLAUSE

Annette Curtis Klause entered the field of young adult novels with a startling story about a contemporary teenage girl whose mother is dying. She meets and is attracted to a three-hundred-year-old teenage vampire, who is on a quest for revenge against his evil brother. Together they learn about love and the acceptance of death. The American Library Association named *The Silver Kiss* a Best Book for Young Adults in 1991.

Combining her interest in science fiction with her inclination toward the supernatural, Klause's second novel—tentatively titled *Going Home*—explores the relationship between a twelve-year-old girl and an alien traveling home to a new planet on a spaceship that is haunted.

Born in Bristol, England, Annette moved with her family to Newcastle-upon-Tyne, the place where "The Hoppins" is set. "I went to that fair every year," she says, "and, when I was fourteen, watched the rough young men who ran the rides with much interest. I never met a werewolf, though."

At fifteen she moved to the United States and currently lives with her husband and five cats in Riverdale, Maryland, where she likes to listen to rock music and attend science fiction conventions. Annette Curtis Klause, who also is head of children's services at the Kensington Park Community Library, says her next novel is likely to be about a werewolf girl.

DONALD R. GALLO

This is the fourth collection of short stories by authors writing for young adults that Don Gallo has compiled and edited. Its highly praised predecessors are *Sixteen, Visions,* and *Connections.* Gallo, a former junior high school English teacher and reading specialist, is a professor of English at Central Connecticut State University, where he teaches courses in writing and in literature for young adults. Among his most recent publications are *Speaking for Ourselves: Autobiographical Sketches by Notable Authors of Books for Young Adults* and *Authors' Insights: Turning Teenagers into Readers and Writers.* Dr. Gallo lives in West Hartford, Connecticut.

SC
FIC
SHO

Short circuits.

$14.08

DATE DUE	BORROWER'S NAME	ROOM NO.
SEP 2 6 '94	James Johnson	Bas
FEB 2 4 '95	Matt Marrandin	Lg
OCT 3 1 '95	Tami Green	Cor.
JAN 0 3 '96	eighia Henry	Ricks

$14.08

SC
FIC
SHO

Short circuits.

WITHDRAWN

MADISON JUNIOR HIGH SCHOOL
DIXON ILLINOIS